"There's Ro...
For The B...

Dom said. "Care for a roll in the canvas?"

"Why did you just ask me that?" Alicia asked angrily.

Dom knew full well what he had to do. Alicia didn't deserve this cavalier treatment, but there seemed no other way to extricate himself from the mess his hormones had gotten him into. "Why do you think? I want to go to bed with you."

"If all you wanted was a tumble, you wouldn't be trying so hard to scare me off," Alicia told him.

"I just asked you to come with me to my tent. Does that sound like I'm trying to scare you off?"

"Yes. It certainly does."

Dom muttered a curse under his breath. Damn, but she was a smart woman. If she looked long enough, she'd find a sad truth—that he was alone in this world, and he'd remain alone. Forever.

Dear Reader:

Welcome to Silhouette Desire – provocative, compelling, contemporary love stories written by and for today's woman. These are stories to treasure.

Each and every Silhouette Desire is a wonderful romance in which the emotional and the sensual go hand in hand. When you open a Desire, you enter a whole new world – a world that has, naturally, a perfect hero just waiting to whisk you away! A Silhouette Desire can be light-hearted or serious, but it will always be satisfying.

We hope you enjoy this Silhouette today – and will go on to enjoy many more.

Please write to us:

Jane Nicholls
Silhouette Books
PO Box 236
Thornton Road
Croydon
Surrey
CR9 3RU

KAREN LEABO
UNEARTHLY DELIGHTS

Silhouette Desire

Originally Published by Silhouette Books
a division of
Harlequin Enterprises Ltd.

*First published in Great Britain in 1992
by Silhouette Books, Eton House, 18-24 Paradise Road,
Richmond, Surrey TW9 1SR*

© Karen Leabo 1992

*Silhouette, Silhouette Desire and Colophon are
Trade Marks of Harlequin Enterprises B.V.*

ISBN 0 373 58631 0

22-9209

Made and printed in Great Britain

KAREN LEABO

credits one of her teachers with initially sparking her interest in creative writing. She was determined at an early age to have her work published. When she was in school, she wrote a children's book and convinced a publisher to put it in print.

Karen was born and raised in Dallas. She has worked as a magazine art director, a freelance writer and a textbook editor, but now she keeps herself busy full-time writing about romance.

Other Silhouette Books by Karen Leabo

Silhouette Desire

Close Quarters
Lindy and the Law

To Earthwatch and my fellow adventurers
on the Maya Costal Traders expedition

One

I'm going to throw up. Alicia Bernard was positively pea-green seasick. She and her four co-workers—all of them more at home in a boardroom than on a boat—had been bumping across the Gulf of Honduras in a tiny, leaky dory for almost two hours. As she was positioned in the front of the vessel, with only a narrow plank for a seat, she'd been repeatedly deluged with waves breaking over the bow, forcing her to keep her eyes clenched tightly closed.

Her plastic rain poncho provided little protection; salt water had crept down her collar and had soaked up from the hem of her jeans so that no part of her anatomy remained dry. Water had even found its way inside her rubber boots.

"That's Coconut Cay, coming into view at two o'clock," came the strident voice of their Creole guide, who piloted the motorized dugout with casual expertise. Heartened by the fact that they were nearing their destination, Alicia cracked her eyes open. She got a fleeting impression of a tiny strip of land covered with palm trees before the sting of salt water forced her to close her eyes again.

The dory relentlessly bumped its way toward the island like a roller coaster car. The motion conspired with the hot sun and the motor's drone, intensifying Alicia's nausea. As they moved into more protected waters, the constant bucking gave way to a smoother gait, but her stomach continued to roll threateningly. She chanced opening her eyes again, relieved to see the island had grown and they were heading into a calm lagoon.

Though her eyes still stung, Alicia could make out the forms of two people standing on the beach, one tall, broad-shouldered and definitely male, the other short and gray-haired.

The moment the boat thudded against the sandy bottom, Alicia was over the side. She alighted in knee-deep water and splashed her way to shore, heedless of the questions barked in her direction. She refused to be sick in front of witnesses.

On dry land she ran for the cover of the dense vegetation that seemed to choke the whole island. Her legs ached from dragging her water-filled boots, but she kept moving until she was sure she was out of sight of the others. Then, with a sigh of relative relief, she leaned her head against the rough bark of a palm tree.

Maybe she wouldn't get sick. Now that her feet were on terra firma, she felt better. She took in great gulps of the hot, moist tropical air as she struggled out of her life jacket and her poncho and shook the salt water out of her blunt-cut black hair.

Perhaps if she changed into some dry clothes and had a few sips of something cool, she would start feeling like herself again. She did not like this lack of control over her body. For that matter she wasn't particularly fond of feeling so far out of her element.

The sequence of events that had led to her landing on this island still astounded Alicia. It had started with a staff meeting, during which virtually nothing had been accomplished because all of the vice presidents at Bernard Office Products, herself included, couldn't stop bickering long enough to get any business done. Then her cousin Skip Bernard, vice president of human resources, had suggested that perhaps the company's key personnel ought to go someplace away from the office, away from their usual responsibilities, so they could iron out the friction that had been marring their recent business relationships.

Eddie J.—Edward J. Bernard III, the company's CEO as well as her and Skip's grandfather—had latched on to this idea with surprising enthusiasm. Skip had envisioned a seminar at a resort, with structured meetings designed to help co-workers improve communications, become better managers—all those gimmicks that personnel managers love. Unfortunately, Eddie J. had seen things differently. He decided instead to send his vice presidents on a Globe Rovers expedition.

"You need to learn the meaning of cooperation," he'd said to them as they'd all stared in shocked silence when he'd announced his plans. "You've gotten so caught up in this corporate b.s. that you've forgotten what's important." And so he'd sent them to a place where cooperation was essential to survival, and life was reduced to its most basic components—food, water, shelter and a hard day's work.

Eddie J. knew the meaning of a hard day's work. He'd gotten his start in engineering with the Army, during World War II. He wanted his employees to learn some of the lessons that their luxurious corporate headquarters in Houston couldn't teach. Because he was a major benefactor to Globe Rovers, which provided volunteers for various scientific expeditions around the world, the organization had been only too pleased to meet Eddie J.'s request that an expedition be found to accommodate his vice presidents.

Though Alicia loved and respected her grandfather, she had hated this plan from the start and hated it more with every passing minute. The Great Outdoors was not her forte.

Dominic Seeger stared in disbelief at the woman's small, retreating figure.

"What the hell was that?" he asked Renaldo, the Creole guide who had piloted the boat full of volunteers.

Renaldo shrugged with his typical boredom. "Seasick," he said. "Since she was the smallest one, I put her in the bow, and the sea was rough today."

"Terrific." It was bad enough that Globe Rovers had forced a group of green volunteers on him, all because some bigwig benefactor had insisted. These corporate stuffed shirts probably didn't want to be here any more than Dom wanted them. But to send him a child, and one with a delicate constitution at that—how was he to contend with her?

Seasick. He'd give her two days before the heat, the bugs and the hard ground got to her. She'd be begging to go home.

Virginia Fleet, his research assistant, was already introducing herself to the remaining four ragged-looking volunteers. Close to sixty, with wispy graying hair and a voice like a Marine drill sergeant, Ginny earned instantaneous respect from the newcomers with a few friendly but definite orders. Soon she had them efficiently unloading the baggage and supplies from the boat.

She was better at working with volunteers than he was, Dom conceded. She had more patience than he did and a knack for explaining the often tricky techniques of their profession.

Still, as the head archaeologist on this dig, he had certain responsibilities. He was just about to step forward and introduce himself when Renaldo touched him lightly on the arm.

"The girl is a beauty. How long before she'll be sleeping in your tent?"

Dom laughed mirthlessly. He had spent three months here last year excavating the remains of the post-Classic Mayan village that once occupied this tiny, mangrove-choked island. During that time he'd kept a careful distance from the women he encountered here, whether they be volunteers from the States or villagers from Punta Blanca. Yet Renaldo had gotten it into his head that Dom was a big-time Romeo.

The misconception had to be Virginia's doing. Ginny, a Ph.D. candidate from University of Arizona, had known Dom for years—first as her mentor and now her boss. She insisted that half the female archeology students were panting over him.

"In the first place she's too young," he answered Renaldo. "In the second place, if I so much as looked at her funny, Ginny would nail my hide to the nearest palm tree."

"She's not so young as you think," Renaldo said, commenting on Dom's first observation and ignoring the second. "She got pretty blue eyes, too."

Dom waved a warning finger at his companion. "Hands off, and I mean it."

Renaldo threw back his head and laughed. "Not me, man. My wife, she slit my throat if I even think about it. But you, now—a young man like you needs a woman. You might like digging up your little bits of junk from the earth, but old pots and bones can't keep you warm at night."

"Who needs warmth in this place?" Dom asked acidly, plucking the front of his damp T-shirt away from his body.

"I thought January was supposed to be the rainy season. Where the hell's the rain?"

Renaldo shook his head and peered off into the distance where the sky held a decidedly gray tinge. "You be careful what you wish for, man. You might get it."

Dom might have made a smart comeback, but a movement at the corner of his vision caught his attention. The woman in question had just emerged from the jungle. She stood at the edge of the clearing by the beach, looking pale but otherwise fit as she calmly assessed her companions unloading the dory and toting the various supplies in the directions Ginny pointed.

Poor thing, he caught himself thinking. She had no idea what she'd gotten herself into. Since no one was paying the girl the slightest bit of attention, he wandered over in her direction. Maybe he could talk her into heading back to the mainland with Renaldo this very afternoon. That would certainly save him the bother of baby-sitting.

"Hello, there," he called out in a deceptively friendly voice. "Welcome to Coconut Cay."

She turned her head sharply, pinning him with startled navy-blue eyes, but then her face melted into a warm smile. She thrust a well-manicured hand in his direction. "Alicia Bernard. You must be Dr. Seeger, the archaeologist."

"Dominic—that is, you can call me Dom," he returned, suddenly conscious of his own work-roughened hand as he took her smooth one. "Renaldo said you're not feeling well."

Her ivory skin pinkened slightly. "The trip from Punta Blanca was something like a roller coaster, only wetter," she replied, glancing down at her damp clothes. "I think I'm okay now, but is there someplace I could change?"

He hoped not. He liked the way she looked in a wet T-shirt. Renaldo had been right—this was no child. Though she was small in stature, she was closer to thirty than twenty, and she bore an air of sophistication that could be gained only through age and experience.

Her glossy black hair, worn in a short, Cleopatra-style pageboy, made him wonder if she was part Italian, like him. Then again, her skin was fair, almost translucent—and looked as if she were accustomed to weekly facials. The white baseball cap perched on her head didn't provide much protection from the punishing sun, either. He glanced down at her hands, again noting the impeccable state of her short but well-shaped nails.

This exotic-looking little orchid didn't appear capable of lifting anything heavier than a bottle of nail polish. She'd probably never done a hard, physical day's work in her life, and she had to pick now to try it.

"No sense in changing into dry clothes," he answered her, glancing at the threatening bank of dark gray clouds gathering in the southeast. "We have a lot of work to get done before dark, and we don't stop because of a little rain."

Alicia groaned inwardly at the thought of grubbing around in wet clothes for the rest of the afternoon, but she didn't argue. It wouldn't be prudent to get any more of her limited wardrobe wet, but that didn't mean she liked the way the archaeologist had made his point. Though his words sounded cordial enough, they were faintly challenging, as if he expected her to object to the suggestion of work.

She surveyed him openly from the feet up, first taking in his battered canvas shoes and tanned legs that looked accustomed to hard exercise. His cut-off jeans and threadbare black T-shirt were remarkable only in their utter lack of style—but then again, fashion didn't appear to be a valuable commodity on Coconut Cay. His shoulders, however, were quite remarkable, wide as a linebacker's, and his hard-looking biceps appeared capable of lifting her right off the ground, if he chose. The raw power she sensed gave her a small, inward shiver of unease.

His face, a blend of features as harsh and unyielding as the elements, was not particularly handsome. Still Alicia found herself fascinated by the tough, untamed look of him. His thick and shaggy dark hair and the reddish stubble of a couple of days' growth of beard provided a sharp contrast to the smooth-cheeked, razor-barbered men she encountered in her day-to-day life—men like her fellow volunteers. Men like the ones she dated, when she dated.

His greenish-hazel eyes were by far his best feature—large, expressive and rimmed by lashes that were obscenely long and thick for a man. Those eyes gave him away. He resented her—didn't want her here at all. Why, when he knew nothing about her?

She took a deep breath. "If there's work to do, why aren't we doing it?" she asked, taking off toward the beach where a stout, gray-haired woman barked out orders.

The woman's lined face softened the moment she caught sight of Alicia. "I was starting to get worried about you, honey. Renaldo said you were sick."

"Now that I'm on solid ground, I'm fine," Alicia assured her as she perched on the edge of the dugout so she could empty the water out of her boots.

"Are you sure? We have all manner of stomach medicine in the first-aid kit."

"I'm sure," Alicia answered with a confident smile. "You're Virginia Fleet?"

The older woman extended her hand. "Ginny. And you must be Alicia. Looks like you and I will have to stick together during the next two weeks if we want to survive this bachelor party."

"Bachelor party?"

Ginny laughed stridently. "That's what I call it whenever we get an all-male volunteer team. Without their women around to temper them, even the most civilized men turn into vulgar Neanderthals in this environment. Something about sleeping in a tent and eating too much fresh fish, I imagine. You can't believe what a challenge it is just to find a private place to bathe when the island is overrun by men with an excess of testosterone.''

"Surely not *these* men," Alicia said, finding it hard to imagine Robert or Del or Peter, or even her cousin Skip, as anything remotely resembling vulgar.

"You watch," Ginny said with a sage nod. "Sure you feel all right?"

Alicia nodded. She sensed, rather than saw, Dom's approach from behind.

"In that case, why don't you and Dom grab some of that lumber and carry it up to the house?''

House? Alicia thought as she reached into the bottom of the boat and grabbed on to the end of a long pine plank. Dared she hope that this island might afford something as civilized as an actual wooden structure? The briefing Skip had prepared emphasized that the volunteers would live in tents.

She expected Dom to grab on to the other end of her board. Instead he selected his own, hoisted it onto his shoulder and took off up the path.

Virginia shook her head. "Macho," she mouthed silently as she helped Alicia with the plank. Together the two women carried it in the direction Dom had taken.

The "house" proved to be a ramshackle three-room structure on stilts with a sagging porch, termite-ridden siding and a sievelike roof.

"Some digs, huh?" Ginny commented as they stacked the plank on a growing pile of new lumber. "Renaldo is going to repair the floors enough that we can use it for lab work. But unfortunately the building won't be fit to sleep in—not if it rains, anyway."

"Speaking of rain . . ."

Alicia jumped at the sound of Dom's voice behind her. Damn, but the man could move quietly.

"Looks like we're finally going to get some," said Ginny as she assessed the darkening sky. "We'd better get all the tents up posthaste."

As soon as Alicia had fetched her poncho and life jacket, she followed the two archaeologists around the house to the area where it appeared their main camp was situated. She paused to observe her four co-workers standing under a palm tree, arguing over who would be partnered with whom in the tiny two-man tents. She was lucky in that respect. As the only woman volunteer, she would have her own private shelter.

"I'll help you with your tent, Alicia," Ginny offered. "I believe Renaldo put you over...there." She pointed to a small clearing on a slight rise, a short distance away from the other tent sites. "Should give you a little privacy, anyway." She started toward the area she'd indicated, but Alicia stopped her with a hand to her shoulder.

"I can take care of it," she said. "I think you'd better straighten out that mess." She nodded toward her four arguing companions before going on about her business.

She'd never erected a tent before, but it didn't look awfully difficult. When she reached the site, she opened the nylon bag Ginny had given her and extracted the poles and stakes. After a moment's study of the illustrated directions she began hooking the poles together to form two intersecting arches, from which she suspended the tent.

As she worked, she was supremely aware of Dominic Seeger's movements about the camp. Even when she wasn't looking directly at him, she knew exactly where he was. There was something about him—a raw virility, perhaps— that both excited and frightened her. She had won over all manner of intimidating and powerful males in the business world. She had played by the rules, and sometimes she'd changed the rules or broken them, to earn a vice presidency at Bernard Office Products. But here on this island, Dominic made the rules, and right now she wasn't sure he even wanted her to play in the game.

Her first instinct had been to meet his resentment with aggression, to show him that she was not to be underestimated. Now she wondered if she shouldn't back down a little. Her grandmother had always told her she would catch more bees with honey than vinegar. Not that she wanted to "catch" Dom, but she did need to convince him that they were on the same side. Otherwise, the next two weeks would be an exercise in frustration.

She felt him approaching as she pushed the final plastic stake into the soft ground with her boot, pulling the nylon taut.

"You've been camping before," he said as he inspected her handiwork.

"Never," she replied. "I always thought it was a waste of time, grubbing about in the woods with tents and sleeping bags. I never have understood why people get on these back-to-nature kicks when they have perfectly good homes and baths with running water." She stopped when she realized she was revealing her resentment to a stranger. Now that she was here, she intended to perform to the best of her ability. Whining about the conditions would serve no constructive purpose.

Dominic stared at her for a moment as if he didn't quite believe her. "You made pretty quick work of this tent."

"I'm an engineer," she answered breezily as she stuffed her duffel and sleeping bag through the tent opening.

"You're an engineer?"

She was used to the note of surprise that always accompanied that question. A female engineer was still something of a rarity. "Didn't you read the bio I sent with my Globe Rovers application?"

"No," he admitted.

"Well, I design office products—tape dispensers, hole punches, staplers, desk lamps—you look disappointed."

He shrugged. "I guess I was hoping maybe you designed bridges or buildings. Something like that might be useful around here. Unfortunately we don't have much call for lamps or tape dispensers."

His cynicism was impossible to miss. For some reason, Dominic was determined not to like her. She struggled for an appropriate comeback, but he drifted away before one came to mind.

An ominous roll of thunder reminded her of the approaching storm. Pushing Dom to the back of her mind, or at least as far back as possible, she climbed inside her tent and arranged her things to her satisfaction. When she was done, she peeked out the flap, not surprised to see that the guys were still struggling with their tents. She could have offered to help them, but that would only wound their male egos, she decided. Instead she would see if Ginny needed help sheltering the supplies and equipment from the rain.

Once again she climbed into her red plastic poncho, just as the first few drops splattered onto the nylon overhead. Ginny did need help, and she instructed Alicia to stack food supplies, dishes and utensils in the one room of the house that didn't have a rotted floor—although half of one wall was gone. A light sprinkle of rain persisted as Alicia carried out her task.

Just as she finished, the rain began in earnest, pouring down in sheets so thick she couldn't see more than a few feet in front of her. Rather than trying to make her way back to her tent, she decided to remain in the dubious shelter of the house until the storm passed. She found a dry spot in one corner, removed her poncho and spread it across the dirty floor, then sat down to wait.

Moments later she heard footsteps on the porch. Dominic appeared in the doorway, looking as if he'd barely escaped the worst of the downpour. He didn't see her at first, and as he shook rain droplets from his hair, Alicia was once again struck by the man's barely suppressed power. Give him a haircut, a shave and a tailored suit, and he'd be hell on wheels in a corporate setting. Without lifting a finger he could intimidate almost anyone.

"What are you doing here?" he asked when he spotted her.

She would try one more time to win him over. She could be charming when she wanted to be. "I was storing the food supplies," she answered, forcing a smile. She'd had years of practice playing politics, and sometimes that meant being nice when it wasn't warranted. "Now I'm just trying to stay dry," she continued. "How long do these downpours usually last?"

"Oh, anywhere from twenty minutes to all day and all night. Sometimes it doesn't stop for days. We might be working in it, sleeping in it, cooking in it. I hope you're not too fond of dry clothes."

"No more than the next person," she said, injecting a note of cheer into her voice as she surveyed the water dripping through the leaky roof. She had managed to avoid the drips, but Dom was fighting them. She patted the rain poncho on which she sat. "This is the only dry corner in the whole place, I'm afraid. You're welcome to join me here."

Dom studied her and the tiny square of red plastic she indicated and abruptly shook his head. He would have liked to avoid the cold rivulets that found their way into his hair and down his neck, but he didn't want to sit that close to Alicia Bernard. He had gone entirely too long without a woman, and this one was small and pretty and she smelled as fresh as a rain-washed flower. She would throw his deprived hormones into an uproar if he let her.

The rain was a stroke of good luck. Though Coconut Cay could feel like paradise when the sun shone and the trade winds rustled gently among the palms, continuous rain could make it a living hell—not the sort of place that would appeal to the likes of the refined woman sitting in front of him. She might still decide to leave, especially if he gave her a few subtle nudges.

"This island isn't quite what you had in mind when you signed up for this trip, is it?" he said casually.

She shrugged. "I wasn't sure what to expect. They told us to be flexible, though, and I can see why."

"You never know what you might meet up with next," he agreed. "I found a centipede in my tent yesterday—but don't worry about that," he continued when her eyebrows flew up. "They're essentially harmless. Well, maybe not harmless, but at least they're not aggressive."

"You mean they run away if given a choice?" she asked.

"Fast as a hundred little legs will take them. Reclusive critters."

"How reassuring," she said dryly.

"Actually I'd rather deal with centipedes than sand flies."

Alicia's upper lip curled in distaste. "I read about those. Aren't they something like mosquitoes?"

"Smaller. In fact, you can hardly see them. They weren't bad today because of the wind. But if the breeze dies, they'll be on you like a plague. They swarm and attack every inch of exposed skin." He paused, surveying her bare throat with casual interest. "I hope you have a scarf of some sort to tie around your neck."

Her hands went unconsciously to the part of her anatomy in question.

Dom decided to push his advantage. "It's not that bad, so long as you're not allergic to the bites."

"What happens if you're allergic?"

"You'll have welts on you the size of nickels. Calamine lotion helps, though. It's not very attractive, but it takes away the sting."

Alicia folded her arms across her raised knees and rested her chin on them, looking thoughtful for a moment. "The work here must be fascinating for you to put up with such hardships for months on end."

That was hardly the reaction he'd hoped for. "Not everyone finds this sort of excavation interesting. In fact, it's a rather dull site when compared to some of the huge Mayan ceremonial centers. After all, we don't have any pyramids."

"Then why do you persist with it?" she asked, sounding genuinely curious.

Dom often wondered that himself. Certainly his father's former interest in the Mayan coastal communities had influenced him. In fact it was Raymond Seeger who first negotiated with Coconut Cay's owner for permission to dig here more than twenty years ago. But somehow the excavation never got under way—not until Dom came here last year.

If he didn't do it, perhaps no one would. He had a certain sense of obligation to finish what his father had started. But he had no desire to go into these explanations with Alicia Bernard.

"I don't mean to downgrade your profession," she continued when he didn't answer, "but what can society hope to benefit by learning about the trinkets some dead civilization traded a thousand years ago?"

"How will society benefit from an improved tape dispenser?" he countered.

"Touché."

"I do this because I love it," he said, answering her honestly. "And I prefer this type of dig to something more glamorous. It's not easy, but there's nothing more challenging or rewarding than finding little bits of the past and putting them together like a jigsaw puzzle—'' He stopped himself. If he wasn't careful, he'd be convincing her to stay instead of go. ''It does take some getting used to,'' he said.

''You mean the climate?''

''The climate, the diet, the work—but I'm sure you can handle it,'' he added, not wanting to be too obvious. ''Just expect a few sore muscles, and blisters. We'll have to clear the excavation site with machetes, which are tough on your hands if you're not used to it. And sometimes it takes the body a while to adjust to the heat and the diet. You do like rice, beans and fish, I hope.''

''It all sounds very healthy to me,'' she said.

''Some people really blossom in this environment,'' he agreed. ''But others . . .''

''Others what?'' she prodded.

''Well, let's just say that a certain percentage of volunteers return to civilization before the two weeks are up.''

''And you think I'll be one of those,'' she concluded, bristling.

He tried to appear surprised at her suggestion. ''The last thing I want to do is scare you off. Of course, Ginny and I can't force you to stay if you decide to hitch a ride back to Punta Blanca with Renaldo, but I try to hang on to as many volunteers as I can.'' *But not if they don't see any value in archaeology,* he almost added.

''I wouldn't *dream* of cutting short my stay on Coconut Cay,'' she said, a little too passionately, causing Dom to wonder who was jerking whose leash. ''I feel it's my obligation to complete the job I signed up for. And surely the feeling of accomplishment will outweigh any minor discomforts.''

He'd underestimated her, Dom acknowledged. Alicia was not about to fall for reverse psychology. If she was determined, she might just prove herself capable of handling this job, despite her inexperience and small stature.

Another cold drip found its way down his collar, and the dry spot next to Alicia looked more appealing all the time. After a moment's deliberation he joined her on the outstretched rain poncho. He searched for something to say, something that would bridge the chasm he himself had put between them. But his thoughts were short-circuited by the sight of something wiggling on top of Alicia's cap.

"Don't move," he said, his tone deadly serious.

"What?"

"I said don't move." He grabbed the bill of her hat and pulled it off her head, then flung it across the room.

"Just what the hell do you think—" she started to say, but Dom was pointing toward the hat.

"Look," he said.

When her eyes finally focused on the large tarantula still clinging to her cap, her face lost all its color. She reached one hand toward him, instinctively grasping his forearm. "That *thing* was crawling on me?" she said in a breathless voice.

Dom was torn. He'd wanted to frighten her a little, but not this badly. He felt an undeniable urge to protect her rather than drive her away. "I forgot to warn you about tarantulas, but they won't hurt you, really," he said. "You must have disturbed this one from his home—no one's been in the house for a while..."

His words trailed off as he reached out to run his index finger down the length of her hair. It was like black silk, thick and shiny as a raven's wing and faintly scented with something mysteriously feminine. He wondered what that softness would feel like against his face.

For one insane moment she looked as if she might respond favorably to his overfamiliarity. Her navy-blue eyes grew even darker and her lips parted in surprise. He leaned closer still, eyeing those soft pink lips.

Abruptly the moment ended. Her eyes narrowed as an expression of understanding came over her features. "If that carnivorous spider doesn't scare me off this island, do you actually believe that sexual intimidation will?"

"But I wasn't . . . I didn't mean—"

She reached up and caressed his hair in a mocking mirror image of the way he'd touched hers. "Next time you'd better be very sure of what you're offering, because you might get more than you bargain for."

It was an excellent exit line, and she used it, despite the fact that rain still poured down by the bucketful.

Dom sat very still for uncounted seconds, horrified at what he'd done and at what she believed he'd done. The impulse to touch her had been something entirely apart from his scare tactics. When she'd been so frightened for those few moments, so vulnerable, all thoughts of getting rid of her had vanished. He'd been consumed with a sudden need to capture some part of her for himself.

He'd meant no harm by touching her, but the gesture had been exceedingly ill-timed. Only moments earlier he *had* been trying to unnerve her a bit, with all the talk of bugs and blisters, and she'd seen through it. It was only natural she would believe his touching her was just another step in his campaign to send her packing. She should have slapped him—slapped him and gotten it over with. Instead she'd neatly turned the tables on him.

Now he was the one shaking in his tennis shoes. Alicia Bernard posed more of a threat to his peace of mind than she'd ever know. And like an idiot he'd opened Pandora's box.

Two

Alicia almost tumbled down the stairs in her hurry to get out of the house and away from Dominic Seeger. The warm tropical rain immediately soaked her to the skin, but it was still at least a full minute before she realized she'd left her poncho behind.

It was another full minute, or perhaps two, before she acknowledged the real reason she was so upset. Dom's less-than-subtle gesture was alarming enough, but her reaction to him was downright terrifying. She should have felt repelled by his touch. Instead her whole body had come alive, almost vibrating in response to his light caress along the length of her hair. It was a wonder she'd come up with that desperate show of bravado.

She leaned against the trunk of a tree and closed her eyes, recalling the moment with a mixture of pleasure and trepidation. For one crazy instant she had actually entertained the idea of kissing him, of taking his face between her hands and tapping into that barely suppressed power.

What would he think, she wondered, if he knew that his touch had actually excited her, rather than scared her? She was more afraid of herself than of him.

Another question troubled her. Dom must want her off this island pretty badly to resort to such caveman tactics. Why?

When she was sure that she had pulled herself together enough that no hint of her turmoil showed on her face, she went in search of her fellow volunteers. She found them easily enough, congregated in the space that the stilts provided under the house. Lately they'd been nothing but a source of irritation for her, but now the sight of their familiar faces buoyed her spirits.

Someone had started a cheery campfire. Alicia worried at first that the house would ignite, but she supposed that because everything was so damp, the danger of an accidental blaze was nonexistent.

"Alicia, there you are," her cousin Skip greeted her. "We're about to have our first 'encounter meeting,' and we need your presence."

The pained expressions of the other three men reflected Alicia's feelings exactly. She despised Skip's tedious, personnel-textbook exercises.

"What are we going to do, get in touch with our feelings?" she asked innocently, surveying the men seated at a makeshift table constructed from an old door resting on two sawhorses. Benches had been created from two-by-fours and plastic buckets. Instead of sitting with the men, she stood by the fire, hoping to dry out her clothes.

As she turned this way and that, submitting various parts of her body to the fire's warmth, she surreptitiously eyed the four men she worked with. Skip, who at thirty was the closest in age to her own twenty-nine years, was tapping his foot impatiently. As vice president of human resources—and a born manipulator—he was in charge of this little tea party. It was his job to see that Eddie J.'s objectives were carried out. Alicia was fond of Skip, despite the almost constant rivalry they'd never quite outgrown, but sometimes she couldn't resist needling him.

Peter Evans was a heavyset blond man in charge of the sales department. His expression clearly indicated that he wished he had better things to do than wait out a monsoon sitting under a house. Alicia could identify with that.

Robert Axel, head of the marketing department, was a thin, dour man in his early forties who could never sit still for long. Now his pale blue eyes darted anxiously from one person to the next, as if he expected someone to pull a rabbit out of a hat and save them all from these unpleasant circumstances.

Then there was Del Gleason—dear, sweet Del, who was near retirement age but who would never, ever leave Bernard Office Products, not unless someone carried him out in a box. Alicia had known him since she'd worked for him on the assembly line as a teenager. He was always unfailingly kind to her, although he had his reservations about women in engineering. Alicia worried about him—worried that this environment might be too harsh for a man his age. But he'd insisted on coming, even though Eddie J. had been perfectly willing to exempt him.

"So what are we discussing?" she finally asked.

"Goals," said Skip. "We know what Eddie J. wants, but what do we, as individuals, want to accomplish on Coconut Cay?"

There was a universal groan.

"Survive and get back home," said Robert.

"Agreed," said Del.

"I'd like to lose a few pounds," Peter ventured. Then they all looked at Alicia, anticipating her answer.

"I'd like to do a good job while we're here," she said, surprising herself as well as her co-workers. "I know the work isn't what we're used to, but I think we should try to be a credit to Bernard Office Products and Eddie J."

"Yes, Pollyanna," Peter muttered.

"Well, I for one question Eddie J.'s motives," Robert said. When the others looked at him, mouths open, he quickly continued. "You all know I have a great deal of respect for the man, for what he's accomplished. But he's getting old. Hell, he *is* old. And he's looking to choose a successor."

"You think he wants to see who's the toughest among us?" Peter asked, obviously intrigued with the idea. "Without our usual corporate structure, without any protocol to fall back on, this experience will separate the men from the boys, right? Uh, sorry, Alicia."

"That's ridiculous," Alicia blurted out. "How would he know how well we perform, anyway? He's not here."

"But he has you, doesn't he?" said Peter. "Couldn't you be his eyes and ears?"

"You think I'm here to spy?" she said. "Right. I'll give him a bad report on all of you, so he'll choose me as his successor." When she saw that they'd taken her seriously, she put a hand to her forehead. She couldn't imagine her grandfather testing them in such a cold-blooded manner. "Are you people nuts? Eddie J. would never pick me to succeed him. I'm too young and I've only been a vice president for two years."

"Oh, really?" said Peter, his voice laced heavily with sarcasm. "Is that why you run around acting like you already own the company?"

An uncomfortable silence followed his question.

"Well, someone had to say it," Peter mumbled defensively.

"Alicia, who do you think Eddie J. *would* pick to succeed him?" Robert asked innocently.

She still shook inwardly over the unfairness of Peter's accusation, but she wasn't about to let any of them know. "I have no idea," she answered breezily. "Believe what you like. If you guys want to scrabble around like a bunch of dogs trying to take charge of the pack, go right ahead, but leave me out of it."

"Can we get back to goals?" Skip pleaded.

"Hey, look, the rain stopped," Alicia said, ignoring her cousin. "Can someone direct me toward the bathroom?"

A round of chuckling greeted her question, which made her distinctly uneasy. Del pointed her toward a path that led off into the jungle.

She followed the path, noticing for the first time the amazing variety of vegetation. There were two different kinds of palms, several types of fruit trees—guava, breadfruit, bananas and sour oranges, she recalled from Skip's painfully thorough report—and mangroves dipping their weird, tangled roots into the water.

She was so engrossed in her study of the flora that she didn't see the outhouse until she was right on top of it. Then she almost cried out in dismay. *Outhouse* was giving it some, since it didn't have walls or a door.

"Good Lord, surely we can do better than this," she muttered. To complain, however, was not in her nature. Long ago she'd learned that the best way to correct an intolerable condition was to fix it herself. She took mental note of what materials she would need to improve the situation. She would ask Renaldo to pick up the supplies in town when he went back, and she would pay for them herself.

She stopped by her tent on the way back to the house, so she could get paper and a pencil to write down her "shopping list," and was horrified to discover that her temporary domicile was a swamp. Apparently rain water had soaked in from the bottom. Her bedroll and duffel bag were dripping.

With a frustrated sigh she started pulling things out of the tent. Maybe she could at least get her bedding halfway dry before she had to crawl into it for the night.

"Want some help?"

Though the voice startled her, Alicia resisted the urge to turn and look at the speaker. Instead she continued her task, suspending a length of clothesline between two trees. "I'm managing just fine, thank you, Dom," she replied evenly.

"You need to dig a trench around your tent," he said, "so the water drains off and away."

"How kind of you to explain," she continued in the same neutral tone. "You might have told me *before* the rain." As she unrolled her sleeping bag, she couldn't help observing him from the corner of her eye. He had changed into a long-sleeved red T-shirt and a pair of jeans worn almost to white. The soft denim hugged his thighs with a familiarity born of many wearings. He had also combed his hair. Except for the stubble on his chin, he looked civilized.

She unzipped the bag and opened it all the way up, then draped it over the clothesline.

"It won't dry before morning, you know," Dom said. "The air is too damp."

"I'll deal with it."

"But you can't sleep in a wet bedroll."

She whirled around to face him, hands on hips. "What do you suggest I do, check in at the local Holiday Inn?"

"Actually, I was going to offer you the use of my tent."

Alicia's jaw dropped. She'd expected a rally from him, but not so quickly. Now she was the one off balance, but only for a moment. A snappy comeback was on the tip of her tongue when he spoke again.

"Wait a minute—that didn't sound quite right, did it. You can sleep in my tent alone. I have a hammock I can use."

Alicia folded her arms and stared hard at Dom, but she still couldn't figure him out. "Is this an honest offer of assistance or some new ploy to get rid of me?" she asked point blank.

He hesitated before answering, running a hand through his dark hair. "I know I was way out of line back at the house. What are the chances that you could forget what happened?"

He must be joking. Forget the feel of his touch, the hot current that had flowed between them for those few electrifying seconds? Not likely. Still, the contrite note in his voice wasn't without some effect on her. As she opened her duffel bag, relieved to see that the contents were dry, she carefully considered his question.

"I'm a reasonable sort, so I might be willing to let bygones be bygones," she said. "But you'll have to answer one question. Why don't you want me here? Is it because you don't think I'm tough enough? Are you afraid I'll be a burden, that I won't do my fair share of the work?"

He gave a frustrated sigh. How could he explain the answer to her when he didn't understand it himself? Still, if it was the only way she'd let him off the hook, he'd have to come up with some kind of explanation. "Do you have a trowel?" he asked. "I'll try to answer your question, but it's going to require a little thought, and I think better when I'm working."

She reached into her duffel and pulled out a small, sharpened hand trowel, one of the required tools for archaeological excavation. She handed it to him with a dubious expression.

"Thanks," he murmured. Then he hunkered down and started to dig a shallow trench around her tent. "You are entirely right. I was trying to persuade you to leave, at first because I thought you couldn't hack it here." With his eyes focused on his work, he found it easier to talk to her.

"At first?" she prompted.

"You've proved yourself capable and adaptable so far. I can't complain. But there's another reason I'm not wild about your presence on the island. I'm attracted to you— very attracted. You're a major distraction, and I can't afford to be distracted from this work. It might not seem important to you—"

She made an impatient noise. "Well, for heaven's sake, put a lid on it!" she said. "We are civilized human beings, despite our rather uncivilized surroundings. We don't have to act on every urge that strikes us."

"I wasn't planning to act on it—really." He looked up at her then, feeling an overwhelming need to see her face. He wasn't explaining the problem very well, and she obviously wasn't comprehending. He returned his attention to his task with renewed vigor. "Just help me out a little, please."

"What do you want me to do? Anyway," she added under her breath, "I doubt anyone would find me attractive after a couple of days without a real bath."

"All I want you to do is reassure me that the feeling isn't mutual. Tell me you wouldn't sleep with me if I were the last man on earth. Tell me about your boyfriend back in..."

"Houston," she supplied.

"Houston, right. Just tell me you don't find me appealing. That ought to work about as well as a bucket of cold water. We can start fresh and everything will be okay. I think."

He waited for her to reply... and waited... and waited. When the silence had stretched to ridiculous proportions, he was forced to admit that she wasn't going to reassure him in any way. He didn't even want to *think* about why.

He forced himself not to look up again until he'd completed the trench. When he did, he found himself alone.

* * *

She should have simply lied to him, Alicia thought when she was a safe distance away from him. It would have made things a lot easier on both of them. But she'd found it impossible to look at those broad shoulders, the muscles rippling beneath the snug T-shirt as he dug her trench, and state that she didn't find him at least ... interesting. Even *interesting* would have been a vast understatement. The man intrigued and excited her—there was no denying it. He was larger than life, like no one she'd ever encountered.

She couldn't give him the reassurance he sought, so she'd walked away.

At loose ends, she made her way back to the house. The guys were arguing over how to stoke the fire in preparation for dinner. Robert wanted to pour kerosene over it, while Peter insisted on following the instructions in his ancient Boy Scout manual. Skip was playing arbitrator, trying to get them to negotiate and compromise.

Fat chance, Alicia mused.

Ginny was there, too, haggling good-naturedly with Renaldo over the price of a string of fish he'd caught.

"You want *how much?*" Ginny asked, arching her eyebrows in feigned shock. "For those skinny little fish?"

"They not skinny," Renaldo argued, as if she'd injured his pride. "It took me all afternoon to catch those snappers, man."

Alicia stared in revulsion at the fish, lying on the makeshift table. She shuddered as one of them wiggled against the stringer that held it captive. Its iridescent scales gleamed even in the fading dusk.

She turned away from the fish and tried not to gag. She despised seafood, and a steady diet of it was something she didn't look forward to.

When Ginny and Renaldo reached a price and she had paid him, she turned to the others. "Now," she said, "which of you big, strong men knows how to clean fish?"

"Alicia knows," Skip piped in helpfully.

Alicia mouthed a silent curse in his direction. Of course she knew. As children, she and Skip had been on more than one fishing expedition together with their grandfather, and the old man had always seen to it that Alicia did her share of the work. She hated cleaning fish now as much as she did then, and Skip knew it. Despite his attempts to settle the vice presidents' differences in a mature fashion, under the surface he was still a kid.

"Would you mind, Alicia?" Ginny asked.

In answer Alicia stood and accepted the sharp knife Ginny held out. She gritted her teeth and swallowed her bile as she cut the heads off, gutted them and clumsily filleted them. Her only revenge was forcing Skip to dispose of the leavings.

Figuring she'd contributed enough to the evening meal, she left the men to cook the fish on a griddle, precariously balanced over the campfire. That ought to cause a whole evening's worth of arguments, she thought as she took a bar of soap and made her way to the water's edge, where she could wash her hands of the fishy smell.

She invented a few tasks to keep her busy and away from the fire, away from the smell of frying snapper, but it was only a reprieve. She'd have to eat the damn stuff sooner or later.

When Ginny sounded the dinner bell, Alicia returned reluctantly to the company of the others. The single table now served as a buffet. She scooped up modest portions of sticky rice and red beans for herself, then added one small, crispy fillet. She was tempted to casually toss the fish into the fire when no one was looking, but if anyone caught her they might lynch her. Food was a precious commodity here on the island, not to be wasted.

Comfortable seating was at a premium, too, Alicia noted. Her companions took up all available space on the unsturdy benches, leaving her the luxury of choosing between a yellow bucket or an orange one. She took the orange one, upended it near the fire, and used it as a stool. She steadied a bottle of Coke between her feet and set her plate in her lap.

To her irritation, Dom chose the other bucket and pulled it up next to her.

"You never answered me," he said casually.

"I've forgotten the question," she lied, as she took a bite of the rice. It was horribly bland. She made a mental note to add spices to her shopping list.

"Do you want to use my tent since yours is wet?" he asked, as if that were the only issue between them. "I can string my hammock up almost anywhere."

"That's very generous of you," she said in her most polite voice.

"What about the other matter?" he asked, changing the subject as casually as if he were inquiring about the weather.

Damn, why couldn't he just drop it? "You were looking for certain reassurances, if I recall," she said carefully as she pushed the fish around on her plate. Then she said, very succinctly, "I can't give them to you."

"Then you're saying that if I made a pass at you, you wouldn't turn me down?"

The bluntness of the question surprised her, although it probably shouldn't have. His game seemed to be comprised of equal parts subtlety and shock value. "Honestly? I don't know what I'd do. But I sincerely hope, for both our sakes, that you won't test me. As I said before, we are civilized people. We don't have to give in to every urge."

"Are you going to eat that fish or play with it?" he asked irritably.

"I was just waiting for it to cool." She popped a piece of the fish into her mouth and chewed, struggling not to let her distaste show on her face. She'd already admitted that she was uncomfortable here. Any further complaints would brand her as a whiner—not the sort of image she liked to cultivate.

Dom tried to study her dispassionately. Surely there was something about her appearance he didn't like. He took inventory, from the shiny cap of black hair glowing in the firelight to the toes of her rubber boots, noting the length of her eyelashes, the curve of her jaw, and the rounded softness of her breasts beneath her blue and white Globe Rovers T-shirt. Nothing about her displeased him. She was as refined and delicate a woman as he'd ever laid eyes on, but he was beginning to sense an inner core of pure steel beneath the dainty exterior.

She looked up and caught his intent gaze. Immediately they both looked away. He wished he'd never come over here to sit with her. By staring at her, he'd only succeeded in becoming aroused.

Since Dom hadn't helped prepare dinner, Ginny pressed him into service washing dishes, using two buckets of cold salt water. As he performed this task, everyone else gathered around the propane lantern to listen to Ginny explain the work they would all be doing the following day. Dom tuned out her words and further tortured himself by again watching Alicia. Away from him she seemed more relaxed, smiling and laughing with the other volunteers. He wondered what he would have to do to get her to be that open with him, then censored the thought.

As soon as everything was in order for the night, he slipped away from the others to get his hammock and knapsack from his tent. He was actually looking forward to a night spent outside under the stars. Renaldo, who had an uncanny talent for predicting the weather, had assured Dom that he could expect a brisk breeze and no more rain, at least until daylight.

The laughter coming from beneath the house had taken on a decidedly boisterous tone. Volunteers were always too keyed up the first night to retire at a reasonable hour. They might remain congregated until after midnight, talking and drinking beer—one of the few luxuries this place afforded. If they were hung over tomorrow, they wouldn't make the same mistake again.

He selected a site well away from the others so that he, at least, could get some sleep. Working in the dark, he strung the hammock between two trees with practiced efficiency, then quickly exchanged his jeans for a pair of soft sweatpants.

As he fished around in his knapsack for his toothbrush, his hand rubbed against the foil wrapping of one of his carefully hoarded candy bars. The others could have the beer, he thought with a grin. He'd take chocolate.

A few minutes later he sank slowly into the hammock. Its old fibers creaked with comforting familiarity, but he knew that the moment he got friendly with it, it could turn on him—literally—and dump him on the ground in the blink of an eye. He carefully arranged his body, then untensed one muscle at a time until he was completely relaxed—for the first time since the volunteers had arrived, he realized.

He was just drifting to sleep when something hit him with the force of a bulldozer, and he fell face first onto the damp earth.

The "bulldozer" was Alicia—her delicate "oomph" had told him that, and she hadn't fared much better than he had. Even in the darkness he could tell she was sprawled beside him, her pale, oval face bearing an expression of utter surprise.

"Dom, is that you?"

"None other. Ever heard of a flashlight?" he asked dryly as he rose to his knees, brushing mud and wet grass off the front of his T-shirt.

"I left it at my tent. I've been back and forth enough times now that I thought I knew my way—I *did* know my way. I just wasn't prepared for a roadblock."

Dom had recovered enough to see the humor in the situation. "You're not hurt, are you?" he asked. When she assured him that she wasn't, he couldn't help laughing. Soon she joined him, and they chuckled foolishly at each other. The laughter diffused some of the tension between them.

"I hate putting you out of your tent—why don't I sleep in the hammock?" she asked him. "You don't seem to be faring awfully well with it."

"It's a tricky beast," he agreed. "But I'm used to it. It takes practice to be able to sleep comfortably in it. And believe me, you'll want a good night's sleep before your first full day of work here."

"What could be so tricky about it?" she asked, sounding definitely affronted that he would impugn her sense of balance. "Let me at least give it a try."

"Be my guest," he said affably, certain that she would end up on the turf just as he had moments ago.

While she examined the hammock, trying to figure out the best means of approach, he reached into his knapsack and extracted the chocolate bar.

"This isn't so bad," she said as she eased herself into a reclining position. "The trick is to lie diagonally, right? That way your back stays straight and you've distributed your weight evenly so it doesn't flip over."

"How the hell did you figure that out?" he asked, wondering if she mastered everything she attempted on the first try. "It took me forever to learn how to lie in it."

"I'm an engineer, remember?" She put her hands behind her head and closed her eyes, appearing completely at ease.

Illuminated only by the faint starlight, she made Dom think of some mythical creature—a nymph sprinkled with stardust, or a fairy-tale princess under a magic spell, awaiting the kiss of her Prince Charming. The illusion was so compelling, in fact, that he had to physically shake his head to rid himself of it.

She shouldn't be here. The moonless, rain-washed evening provided too romantic a setting. He flat out didn't trust himself alone with her, not when they were cloaked in this velvety night.

He distracted himself by unwrapping the candy and breaking off one small square. "Want some chocolate?"

Her eyes opened slowly. "Hmmm?"

"Chocolate." He held the square out to her.

"What, a peace offering?" But she took the candy, examining it suspiciously before putting it into her mouth. Almost magically her expression changed from one of skepticism to sheer bliss.

He watched, fascinated, wondering if that's how she looked when she made love.

"Mmm, heaven," she said. "I thought I'd have to go two whole weeks without a chocolate fix. I wanted to bring some with me, but I was afraid it would melt all over my bag."

"You can buy chocolate in Punta Blanca," he told her.

"Wonderful. I'll add it to my shopping list."

"What shopping list? There's no Bloomingdale's in P.B., you know."

"Just a few things I'm asking Renaldo to bring back from the village tomorrow—if he has time and room in the boat. So how about it? Can I sleep here tonight?"

"Uh, no, Alicia. It's not safe for you to sleep out in the open by yourself. Sometimes we have visitors at night—

trespassers who want to steal food or tools, or even artifacts. They think that just because we're digging here, we're
finding gold and jade.''

Alicia sighed. ''Oh, all right. I guess I'll sleep in your
tent.'' But she made no move to leave.

''Want another bite before you go?'' he prompted, dangling a square of the candy bar before her face.

She nodded, taking the piece of chocolate from his fingers. ''Watch out. You keep bribing me with sweets, and I
might decide you're an okay guy.'' But she softened the barb
with a tentative, fleeting smile just before tossing the candy
into her mouth.

She closed her eyes and sighed happily, savoring the bit of
chocolate.

The temptation was too much for Dom. Without a
thought as to the consequences, he leaned over and brushed
her gently pursed lips with his.

The contact was soft as a raindrop and lasted only the
briefest of moments, but nonetheless he sensed a welcoming from Alicia. He cupped her jaw in the palm of his hand,
and she tipped her chin up and parted her lips slightly in
unmistakable invitation.

This time he took full possession of her mouth, pouring
into the kiss every ounce of the passion he'd been holding in
check. Her response was as untamed as the jungle itself, as
warm as the humid night air that surrounded him, stealing
the breath from his body. She tasted of chocolate and a
thousand forbidden pleasures. When she reached up to
touch his hair, there was no mockery to the gesture.

She was so very alive, so vibrant, like the brilliant blaze
of a match, and he wanted to be closer to her, to draw her
small, warm body next to his and burn himself in her fire.
He couldn't remember ever feeling that way about a woman.
He'd craved physical closeness, and sometimes he found
that—usually with a willing woman he knew he'd never see

again. But this need to be a *part* of someone was new, and not necessarily welcome.

Deliberately closing off the analytical part of his brain, he eased himself down beside her in the hammock and slipped his arm beneath her shoulders. He pulled her against him— and for one shocking instant he was airborne. Then he hit the wet ground, and she landed squarely on top of him.

The bone-jarring collision must have knocked some sense into his head, because he was immediately hit with a sobering awareness. What the hell was he doing? Exactly what he'd promised her, and himself, he wouldn't do. He knew he had to stop the events he himself had set in motion, but he didn't know how. In the end he chose the surest route—also the lowest.

"There's room in my tent for both of us," he said, hoping against hope that she would refuse him. "Care for a roll in the canvas?"

Abruptly she pushed herself up and off him. Obviously he'd succeeded, he'd made her angry. Bravo, Seeger, he congratulated himself without much enthusiasm.

"Why did you say that?" she asked as she stood and brushed the mud from her jeans.

Dom sat up and pulled his knees toward his chest, knowing full well what he had to do, for his own good and hers. She didn't deserve this cavalier treatment, but there seemed no other way to extricate himself from this mess his hormones had gotten him into. "Why do you think I said it? I want to go to bed with you."

"Oh, Dominic, knock it off," she said harshly. "If all you wanted was a tumble, you wouldn't be trying so hard to scare me off."

"I just asked you to come with me to my tent. Does that sound like I'm trying to scare you off?"

"It was the way you asked. And yes, it certainly does."

He muttered a curse under his breath. Damn it, but she was a perceptive creature. If she looked long enough, she would find a sad truth—that he was alone in this world and he would remain alone. Getting close to Alicia was the first step in caring for her, and caring for any woman could destroy his career and unravel the very threads that formed his life. His father had shown him exactly how. And though Raymond Seeger had learned to reconcile what he'd given up, Dom already knew he couldn't.

"Dom?"

"Go away, Alicia. I don't want to have this conversation."

Three

Alicia couldn't remember ever feeling so frustrated. The man kissed her from the very depths of his soul. There was passion, yes, but also tenderness, affection and an endearing uncertainty. No kiss had ever been more compelling or had made her feel more beautiful, more desirable. He had been well on the way to thoroughly enchanting her.

And then he'd popped off that crude proposition.

What prompted him to send out such mixed signals? Did she really want to know?

It wasn't too late, she decided, to wrap herself in righteous indignation and walk away. In two weeks she would be gone from his life. His reasons for such bizarre behavior, whatever they might be, could remain his own.

"Well, then, good night," she said in a deliberately haughty voice. Let him think he'd finally succeeded in scaring her off. He had, in a way. Those raw emotions she sensed just beneath Dom's macho posturing were pretty damned intimidating.

Back at her tent she reached into her duffel bag and retrieved a handful of things she would need for the night. Maybe she was letting her imagination run away with her, she mused. How could she read so much of Dom's emotions from one kiss?

Real or imagined, she'd responded to them—oh, God, how she'd responded. She'd never kissed anyone like that. She'd had her share of involvements, but the men she'd chosen in the past had a certain "safeness" about them. She'd given only a part of herself to them, and none had ever demanded more. But with Dom she had no control over what she gave and what she kept. She gave it all, no questions.

Maybe the heat and humidity had short-circuited her brain. Certainly the climate had already driven her normally dignified co-workers batty—they were under the house even now, swilling beer, smoking cigarettes and swearing like sailors. All she could hope was that morning would bring an end to the insanity. Maybe in the clear light of day, her encounter with Dom could be written off as insignificant.

His tent brought her little comfort, other than the fact that she could finally get out of her damp clothes and into a dry cotton sleep shirt. For one thing the tent reminded her of *him*. As she lay on top of his sleeping bag, for it was too hot to crawl inside it, all she could think about was that he had lain here, too. And when she wasn't thinking about that, the noises of the island kept her awake—weird shrieks and rumbles and flappings, and things that sounded big as elephants moving through the vegetation.

Some primitive segment of her brain wanted more than just the trace of Dom's presence. She wanted him there to protect her from the fearful night things.

Finally she did sleep, but the gray dawn brought a new horror—more rain. When she heard the first drops tapping hesitantly against the nylon, overhead, her first thought was of Dom and the rude awakening he would get. Her second thought was for her sleeping bag. It must be almost dry by now—she couldn't let it get soaked again.

The rainfall was still just a light sprinkle, but in moments it might start pouring. Heedless of modesty, she shoved her feet into her rubber boots and dashed outside, intending to save her bedroll at any cost.

Apparently the same inspiration had struck Dom. By the time she arrived at her tent he was already there, stuffing her things inside.

"Thank you," she said when he'd zipped the flap shut.

He looked up, surprised to see her. His gaze flickered over her bare legs, revealed by the short nightshirt, and then to the boots. "Nice getup," he said with a teasing smile. But at her serious expression he sobered, also. "I didn't mean to be so abrupt last night. It's just that—"

She held up a hand to stop him. "Please, let's just drop it. I'll be done with your tent in a few minutes and you can have it back."

She turned quickly and marched away, her boots squish-squashing in the mud. She could feel his eyes on her, but resisted the temptation to turn and look over her shoulder.

By the time she was dressed and more or less ready to face the day, the rain had stopped. The sun was actually peeking through the clouds as she made her way to the gathering area under the house.

She was the last to arrive for breakfast. Dom and Ginny were busy checking equipment. The others were milling about, looking shockingly rumpled, unshaven, bleary-eyed and utterly useless. She'd be willing to bet at least some of them were hung over.

"Alicia, look at you!" said Skip when he spotted her.

"Look at me what?" She peered down at herself, but saw nothing amiss with her clothes.

"You could've just stepped off the pages of an L. L. Bean catalog," he replied. "The hat, the boots—and what's that camouflage thing strapped around your waist?"

"It's a day pack," she answered indignantly. "I have everything I'll need—tools, gloves, canteen, sunscreen, pocket knife—"

"Manicure set, perfume—"

"Dental floss and breath mints—"

"Don't forget your beeper and your Rolladex—"

She glared at them until they stopped snickering. "I like to be prepared. Do I smell coffee?"

"In that old tin pot sitting by the fire," Del answered her. "Careful, it's hot. We've already had one casualty this morning."

"Someone was hurt?"

"Peter burned his hand," Skip supplied, sounding just like the tattletale she remembered from childhood.

Alicia directed a concerned look toward the large, blond man who slumped at one end of the table. "It's not bad, I hope," she said.

"Bad enough." He held up his bandaged right hand for her to see. "Dom said I have to go back to Punta Blanca with Renaldo and see the doctor there. At any rate, I can't do any digging. Looks like this expedition will have to get along without me, at least for a day or two."

Alicia made some appropriately sympathetic remark, though she suspected Peter was not as glum as he acted. He didn't like it here, and might welcome an excuse to escape, regardless of what Eddie J. might think.

Skip, in an uncharacteristically gallant gesture, poured Alicia's coffee for her. When he handed her the plastic cup, he leaned over to whisper, "That's one down. Who do you think will come out on top?"

She didn't dignify the question with an answer. Instead she lifted the lid on a large pot sitting on the coals, hoping to discover something tasty, like oatmeal. Instead she found last night's leftover fish.

She slammed the lid back down, horrified. "Is that breakfast?" she hissed to Skip.

"Can't let it go to waste, now, can we?" he answered cheerfully. "Say, where were you last night?"

She froze, feeling unaccountably guilty. "What do you mean?"

"You didn't stick around to play poker with us."

"Was it a bonding experience?" she teased. "Did I miss out on an opportunity to learn better communication through bluffing? No, thanks. I went to bed early." She sat on one of the benches to drink her coffee.

Skip settled next to her. "Where were you *really?*" he asked in a voice just loud enough for her to hear. "I paid a visit to your tent around midnight, just to be sure you weren't sick again, and, uh, you weren't there."

"Oh, for Pete's sake. I was in Dom's tent. There, now, are you happy?" She enjoyed her cousin's unabated shock for a few moments before adding, "My tent was wet and Dom offered me his. He slept elsewhere. Now close your mouth before the flies get in."

He grimaced. "Don't say that word."

"What word?"

"Flies. Sand flies. I hope you have plenty of bug repellent in your pack. You should be wearing long sleeves."

"In this heat?" But everyone else was, she noted. And she'd left the insect spray at home because it made her break out in a rash. Oh well, she thought as she spread some peanut butter on a slice of bread. The insects hadn't bothered her yet.

Del sat off by himself, his gray head bent low as if he were pondering something serious. After she'd finished her bread and peanut butter, which tasted like heaven compared to the alternative, she refilled her coffee and joined him. "Is everything okay?" she asked.

"Not really," he answered in a low voice, and without his usual ready smile. "You can't imagine what sleeping on the hard ground does for my arthritis. I don't see how I can do the work they want us to do—all that lifting and bending. Fact is, I was thinking of heading back with Renaldo and Peter when they leave for Punta Blanca."

"You mean you're going home?" It was bad enough that Peter was leaving, but Alicia was crushed at the thought of losing Del.

"This is a place for young people," Del said, sounding defeated. "I was wrong to insist on coming."

"But I don't want you to leave. Dom told me it takes a few days to get accustomed to the food and the climate. You'll feel better in a day or so. Anyway, if you leave, who will defend me against the bozos?" She nodded her head toward Skip and Robert. "You're the voice of reason among us."

She was gratified when he laughed. "That'll be the day when you can't defend yourself. One icy stare from you and they'll toe the line."

"But, Del—"

"I'll make a fool of myself."

"No you won't—I'll help you out," she said emphatically. "We'll stick together, you and me, and we'll help each other. That way no one will know if one of us is wimping out. Try it for one day, please?"

He was silent for a long moment. Finally he nodded reluctantly, then flashed her a conspiratorial smile. In the old days, when she'd first started working for her grandfather's company, Del had more than once covered up blunders she'd made and had gone out of his way to make her look good in front of Eddie J. Now she could return the favor.

Alicia spread out her beach towel on a smooth, flat rock that protruded from the water. With a sigh of exhaustion she eased herself down on the towel, relieved to see the end of her first full day of work on Coconut Cay. How would she survive thirteen more just like it? She was sore in places she hadn't imagined could get sore.

Skip, Robert and Dom were engaged in a spirited game of Frisbee in the shallow lagoon. The three of them had spent the day away from the main excavation, performing some mysterious tasks on the swampy south end of the island. They had returned only a few minutes ago, looking like abominable mud men, and had headed immediately for the water. Alicia, feeling hot and gritty herself, had joined them for just long enough to get wet, but now she was too tired to move a single muscle.

She observed the game for a time, but even that seemed taxing, especially watching Dom. The sight of his powerful body moving gracefully through the water reminded her of the ecstasy they'd touched so briefly last night, and she found herself restructuring the scene a dozen different ways. Realistically she knew she'd done the best thing by walking away, but that didn't stop her from musing about other possibilities.

With a groan she forced her gaze, and her thoughts, to safer subjects.

She'd done well with her efforts to spare Del from the more punishing physical tasks. At least he wasn't talking about going home anymore. And though the work had been exhausting, she had derived a certain fulfillment from her accomplishments.

Even the two hours she'd spent clearing vegetation from the excavation site had been rewarding in the way only hard physical labor could be. She had swung her machete with a vengeance, decapitating small palm trees and decimating large, clinging vines like a demented Samurai warrior. To pause and see the vast area she had cleared with her own hands had been surprisingly satisfying.

The exacting process of measuring the cleared area with survey equipment and marking off a grid with stakes and strings was less strenuous, but undeniably tedious. "I don't think Indiana Jones ever measured anything," she'd commented dryly, earning a brief smile from Del. But when they finished that task they were allowed to begin digging, and she found she really enjoyed herself.

The main excavation site—called Dog Tooth Mound for reasons no one could remember—was incredibly rich. Ginny, Del and Alicia had used sharpened trowels to carefully shave away layers of dirt, and with almost every handful removed they found pottery shards and shiny black obsidian blades, carved razor sharp. The afternoon had taken on the mood of a treasure hunt, with Alicia and Del competing to see who could come up with the best find. Perhaps they weren't taking the work as seriously as they should, but it was hard to be serious about digging ditches when she could think of a million things she ought to be doing back home at the office.

Alicia frowned as she recalled the only disturbing incident to the otherwise tolerable day. She and Del had been digging in the same square, putting the dirt they removed into a bucket. Whenever the bucket became full, she would wait until Ginny's attention was elsewhere, then jump to her feet, pick up the heavy bucket and race with it to the large, course screen that was suspended from a three-legged frame. Then she would hoist the bucket up and dump the dirt in the screen, to be sifted for any artifacts that might have been missed.

Each time she did it, Del would smile in amusement and shake his head over the effort she put forth to save wear and tear on his joints while preserving his pride, as well.

"You work here just like you do at the office," he had commented as together they searched the screen for dime-sized bits of pottery.

"What do you mean?" she'd asked, seeing no similarity between her current activities and those at Bernard Office Products.

"You rush around doing whatever needs to be done, or whatever you *think* needs to be done, whether it's your responsibility or not. But at least here on the island your efforts are appreciated." He'd said the last with a chuckle, and Alicia knew he'd made the comment in all innocence. But she'd stewed about it the rest of the day, pondering the implications.

Sometimes she did meddle in other departments besides her own, whenever she saw that something needed attention, and often her efforts were *not* appreciated. But she had no patience with the slow-moving corporate channels she was supposed to use—channels that were stymied even further by the company's recent rapid growth. She saw no problem with cutting through red tape whenever she could. She'd always thought the ends justified the means.

But if even Del, her friend and usually her ally, could find fault with her, maybe she ought to give it some thought. Maybe her co-workers had a right to be irritated with her.

It was a sobering realization. She had come on this trip feeling sure that the friction among Bernard's VPs was no fault of hers.

A splash of water hit her in the face, forcing her back to the here and now. The Frisbee had splatted against the water right by her rock. She reached for the errant disk, intending to return it to the players, when a long, tanned arm reached for it at the same time.

Alicia relinquished her grip on the Frisbee as soon as she realized who was on the other end of the tussle. Slowly she raised her eyes, taking in the tautly muscled body, revealed all too well by indecently short cut-off jeans and nothing else. The wet denim rode low on his lean hips and clung with exacting thoroughness.

She forced her gaze up, past his chest, his wide shoulders, and finally to his face. What she saw there was hardly comforting, for his expression only mirrored the sudden hunger that gnawed inside her. She nervously adjusted the strap of her swimsuit, which felt much too skimpy.

Dom carelessly flipped the Frisbee toward the other two men, his eyes never leaving Alicia. Without warning he sat down on one corner of her rock, the game forgotten.

"So, how was your first day of working on the mound?" he asked.

She stared up at the azure sky, finding it much easier to talk to him if she didn't have to look at him. "Exhausting. Educational." She couldn't muster enough energy for more answer than that.

He touched one of her hands, then gently uncoiled the fingers she'd unconsciously clenched into a fist. "You're obviously not afraid of hard work," he said, lightly running his thumb over the blisters that riddled her once-smooth palm. "I was wrong to think you couldn't handle the job."

She suppressed a pleasurable shiver. "I'm not ready to run home, if that's what you mean."

"There's some antibiotic cream—"

"Yes, Ginny already showed me where it is."

A long silence followed, and Alicia hoped that Dom would take the hint and leave her alone. Of course, on an island this small they couldn't avoid each other for long. But she wasn't ready to face him now. She was tired and hungry, and her mind felt fuzzy around the edges.

She didn't get her wish.

"You know what I thought when I saw you lying here on this rock?" he asked, still holding her hand.

She sighed. "I can't imagine."

"I thought you looked like a siren, ready to lure unsuspecting sailors to their death with your song."

"I can't sing," she quipped, trying to hide her surprise at seeing this lyrical side to him. "You know, if you're trying to convince me that you're a lecherous lout, you're not doing a very good job. Comparing me to a siren is rather unloutlike. In fact, it's kind of poetic."

"Yeah, well, that's me, I guess. Mr. Poetic." He didn't sound at all pleased with her assessment.

"Come on, admit it," she said, sure she was onto something. "If you didn't have at least a little romance in your soul, you wouldn't have chosen archaeology as a career."

She thought she saw the briefest flash of discomfort cross his face, but he immediately resumed a casual expression, shrugging carelessly. "We're a real romantic bunch, all right. You should meet my father." A trace of sarcasm laced his answer.

"Your father's an archaeologist, too?"

Dom nodded. "Or rather, he was. Now he teaches."

"And what makes him such a romantic?"

Dom shrugged again, not quite so casually this time. "It's not important." He took a deep breath. "What matters is that once again I find myself apologizing to you."

"What for? Oh, for last night," she said, answering her own question. "Now why would you apologize for propositioning me like I was some street-corner trollop?" she asked, her voice saccharine sweet. "After all, you made me really angry, angry enough to walk away, and that's what you wanted. Right?"

He refused to meet her gaze. "It's what I wanted at the time," he admitted. "But I can't leave it alone. I don't want you thinking I'm . . . like that."

"Like what? A jerk? Convince me otherwise," she said, knowing the challenge lacked real conviction.

"Wait a minute—I thought you said I was romantic."

"I suppose there is such a thing as a romantic jerk," she retorted, but she knew she'd lost ground. This was a ridiculous conversation, anyway, she thought as she felt the corners of her mouth tightening in the beginning of a smile.

"Are you sure you don't want to go home?" he asked. "You're the apple in my Garden of Eden, you know."

"There you go, getting all poetic on me again. But I'd hardly call this clammy, muddy, bug-infested island the Garden of Eden. And no, I won't go home until the two weeks are up."

"You don't want to disappoint your grandfather, I suppose. You think he'll choose you to succeed him?"

"Ah, you've been listening to the guys, I see." She grew serious again. "My fellow veeps have feathers for brains. Eddie J. isn't near ready to retire. And if he were, he would no more choose me to run his company than . . . than you." She couldn't think of anyone less appropriate than Dom to head a corporation. "But I still don't want to disappoint him. He has a lot of faith in me. Not only that, but I intend to complete my obligation here for my own satisfaction. I find the work here…challenging." Challenging in a way her work at Bernard wasn't. Already she was learning some startling things about herself. "I'm sorry if my presence here makes you uncomfortable."

"*Uncomfortable* isn't the word," he said, suddenly intense. "Alicia, I want you in the worst way. I've tried to talk myself out of it, but I can't. I want you, and if you don't do something to stop me, I'm going to have you."

Her heart did an unsteady jig and her palms grew moist. He hadn't said it in pretty words, but the sincerity behind the words he'd chosen had a more profound effect on her than endless verses of poetry could. This was nothing like his horrid proposition of the night before. This was from some place deep inside him, and tempting in a way she wouldn't have believed possible.

Before she could respond, she had to see his eyes. She'd been studiously avoiding his gaze, but now she deliberately met it—and wished she hadn't. Just as she had last night when they'd kissed, she felt a nearly tangible jumble of emotions pouring out of him. She could see them in his hazel eyes as clearly as if they'd been inscribed in stone—a yearning so powerful it overrode almost everything else, tempered by a gut-twisting fear.

Why did the very idea of intimacy torture him so? A wild part of her wanted to drag him off into the jungle and make love to him until this crazy desire that had sprung up between them was quenched. Maybe then he would stop looking at her that way. But she had a hunch that making love would only add to the demons that plagued him.

She pulled her hand out of his grasp and sat up as she came to a decision. "I'm flattered," she said, again diverting her gaze from his. "No, I'm more than flattered. I'm overwhelmed. But you must see how impossible this is. A stolen kiss is one thing, but what you're suggesting . . ."

"Is nothing you haven't thought about," he said, running the tip of his finger along her full lower lip.

His touch muddled her logic, and she had to struggle to marshal her shattered thoughts. "But there's no privacy on this island," she said, latching on to her strongest argument. "I'm here with all of my grandfather's company executives, and I don't care to share my personal life with them. You see Skip and Robert?" She nodded toward the two men, still engaged in a half-hearted game of toss. "They're already curious, wondering what we're up to."

She shook her head, the action almost a shudder. "No, I couldn't stand for them to know the intimate details of my life."

"Then you're . . . turning me down?"

Much as it pained her to do so, she nodded. "For real this time." But when she saw the relief that mingled with disappointment on Dom's face, she knew she'd done the right thing.

Suddenly he laughed, then bent down and splashed her with a handful of water.

She reached down and splashed him back.

Not to be outdone, he scooped her up and dropped her into the shallow water, then ran like hell before she had a chance to retaliate.

Alicia could only shake her head in wonder as he waded to shore, laughing at her. The man was crazy, acting like she'd just given him a reprieve from the guillotine.

He was also the most wildly handsome, sexiest man she'd ever come close to, she admitted with a wistful sigh. If he used even a small portion of his persuasive powers on her, in a flash her *no* could turn into a *yes*.

She hoped he never found that out, for it would give him a great deal of power over her. Already she had proved far too susceptible to his sensual pull, revealing more of herself than was wise.

Four

Alicia awoke at dawn to the sound of something scritch-scratching against the nylon of her tent, close to her head. She bolted upright, tensed for battle. The scratching stopped, then started again.

"Hello? Who...who's out there?" she demanded in a shaky voice. But the *thing* didn't sound human.

Alicia wasn't going to let disaster catch her in her jammies this time. She performed a quick wash with a moist towelette—thank goodness she'd thought to bring those—then covered herself with moisturizer before pulling on a pair of white jeans and a T-shirt.

She mentally prepared herself to face whatever was out there, then unzipped the tent flap and peered out. There, at the edge of her tent, was the hugest crab she'd ever seen—big as a dinner plate. It was a disturbing sight, but nothing to panic over, she decided. As she pulled on one boot, she wondered idly if the land crabs around here were edible. Crab meat was surely better than fish.

How would she catch it? she wondered, pulling on the other boot. If she had something to throw over it... Apparently it read her thoughts, because in an instant it had scuttled down its cavelike hole, a few feet away.

Alicia wrinkled her nose as she crawled out of the tent and closed the flap behind her. Two days ago she couldn't have imagined herself wanting to kill something and eat it. This island was doing strange things to her.

She headed for the space under the house, which had become a kitchen, dining hall and recreational area, surprised to see that almost everyone else was already up, dressed and busy. Renaldo, who had spent the night in Punta Blanca, had returned with more supplies, including the canvas and rope Alicia had requested, she noted with satisfaction. She wondered if he'd also remembered the spices and chocolate bars. She looked around for him, intending to ask, but her gaze landed on Dominic instead, and she almost tripped over her own feet.

He was building another sifting screen, working shirtless in a patch of sunlight near the house. The sun glinted off his dark hair and shone on the stubble that shadowed his jaw. She'd seen his bare torso before, but the sight of those powerful shoulders, gleaming slickly in the sun, still caused a quivering beneath her ribs.

He looked up and fixed her with a lingering, regretful gaze before returning his attention to his work.

Alicia quickly busied herself by pouring coffee, hoping her slight sunburn disguised the blush that undoubtedly tinged her face. She'd thought the matter between herself and Dom had been settled, once and for all, yesterday. But each time he looked at her with those emotion-packed hazel eyes, or spoke to her even innocently, she felt her resolve crumbling.

Back in Houston she probably would have given him no more than a passing, appreciative glance. She couldn't imagine herself going out to dinner with him at a fancy restaurant or sitting next to him at the opera.

But here, where he was so much a part of this world, part of the island itself, she was inexorably drawn to him, to the excitement and strength he represented. This place frightened her a little. He made her feel safe.

"Something wrong?"

Alicia jumped, sloshing a few drops of coffee over the rim of her plastic mug. "Oh, hi, Skip. Guess I'm just not quite awake yet," she fibbed. She took a quick inventory of her co-workers, noting the one absence. "Where's Robert?"

"He was up all night, scratching," said Skip, who was Robert's tent mate. "I let him sleep this morning."

Ginny glanced up from the powdered milk and water she was mixing. "Did he try the calamine lotion?"

"Gallons of it. He's head-to-toe pink," Skip said.

"Why's he scratching?" Alicia wanted to know.

They all stared at her. "Sand flies," Del said. "Don't tell me they're not bothering you."

She shrugged. Some of the pesky little insects had been lurking around her tent this morning, she told them, and a few had buzzed around her face, but she hadn't been bitten.

"You're kidding," Ginny said as she slapped at one of the insects in question. "What sort of bug repellent are you using?"

"I'm not using any," Alicia confessed. "It gives me a rash." Her admission was met with another round of shocked stares.

"Are you putting anything on your skin?" Ginny persisted. "The bugs like some people better than others, but I've never known anyone who was completely immune."

Alicia thought for a moment. "Just moisturizer."

By this time, Dom had sauntered up and was listening in on the conversation. "That might be it," he said. "Alicia, can we try some of your moisturizer?"

She laughed inwardly at the thought of all these macho men trailing the scent of "mountain meadow wildflowers," but if they wanted to try it, she was willing to share. "It's in my tent," she said. "I'll go get it."

She smiled as she crossed the campsite, feeling inexplicably cheerful now that she was waking up a bit. She was more rested today than yesterday, at least, and she was pleasantly aware of her body as her muscles stretched their way out of their morning stiffness. The air was clean, and the ocean reflected a clear, aqua blue as the rising sun's rays struck the water. She almost looked forward to the work ahead of her.

Her optimism was interrupted by a low moan. She paused, straining her ears, thinking perhaps she'd imagined it, but then she heard it again, more distinct this time. It was coming from Robert's and Skip's tent.

"Robert?" she called through the screening.

"Alicia?" His voice was faint and thready. Heedless of propriety, she unzipped the tent flap and looked inside. Robert was in his sleeping bag, despite the undeniably warm temperature, and he was shivering. His face resembled a lumpy, pink balloon, and he breathed in shallow, wheezy gasps.

"I'll get help," Alicia immediately said. There was no doubt in her mind that Robert was very ill, perhaps gravely so. She took off toward the house at a dead run.

She headed straight for Dom. In her haste she kicked over an empty bucket and nearly launched herself headlong into his arms.

He smiled, obviously amused. "What's chasing you?"

"Robert's sick," she said, breathless more from panic than exertion. "He's swelled up and feverish—"

Dom's smile disappeared. "Sounds like he's had a reaction to the fly bites. Ginny, get the epinephrine from the first-aid kit," he ordered curtly, even as he gave Alicia's shoulder a reassuring squeeze. "Renaldo, you get the boat ready for a return trip. Skip, come with me. You can help me get him dressed and into the boat."

Everyone moved with amazing efficiency, leaving Alicia standing by the campfire feeling helpless. "I guess we should just stay out of the way, huh," she said to Del, surprised to hear her own voice shaking. She'd never been this close to a medical emergency before.

Del patted the seat next to him on the bench. "Sit down and have some coffee," he said. "I'm sure he'll be fine. From the looks of things, Dom and Ginny know exactly what to do."

Alicia did as Del suggested, quelling her panic by keeping her hands and her mind occupied. "Are you feeling better this morning?" she asked, frenetically stirring her coffee.

"Sore as all get-out, but I did sleep good last night," he said. "I hope I'm not the next one to go. We're dropping like flies—oops, bad choice of words."

"Del!" She nudged his ribs with her elbow. But she had to acknowledge some truth in his words. "As a group we aren't faring awfully well. I guess Peter's not coming back."

"No. Renaldo took him to the airport yesterday."

"You don't believe that nonsense about Eddie J. testing us to see who's the toughest, do you?"

Del shook his head. "I've known Eddie for a lot of years. Longer than you, even. He doesn't play games like that. Still, there's something inside me that wants to make him proud—and that has nothing to do with wanting to take over the company."

"I know exactly what you mean," she said. "He's so damn tough himself, I just hate to think I can't live up to the standards he's set."

Del lowered his voice, though there was no one around to hear. "Off the record, who do you think Eddie J. wants to succeed him? I'm too old, you and Skip are too young—that leaves Robert and Peter."

"Between those two, I'd put my money on Robert," she said, confident that her admission would never be repeated. "But if you want to know the truth, I think he's been grooming you for the job."

"Me?" Del gave a short, self-derisive laugh.

"Age never stopped him, so I don't think he'll hold that against you. Once he retires, I can't think of anyone I'd rather work for than you."

Del grinned, obviously pleased. "Thanks. That means a lot."

They were relieved to see Robert exiting his tent a few minutes later, dressed and walking, though he leaned heavily on Skip's arm. Within seconds the dory's outboard motor coughed to life.

"I think I'll go see if I can't finish that screen Dom was working on," Del said as he eased himself off the bench. He declined her offer of help and left her sitting at the table alone, nursing her coffee and feeling a bit useless.

As soon as the others returned from launching the boat, she jumped reflexively to her feet. "Is Robert going to be all right?"

"He'll be fine," Dom assured her, noting with concern the pallor beneath the slight sunburn that pinkened her nose and cheeks. As he slid onto the bench across from her, he searched for something to say that would erase the worried frown from her face. "The epinephrine took effect almost immediately. His breathing was much better by the time we got him on the boat. The swelling should start to go down within a few minutes."

"That's good to hear," she said, sinking back down on the bench. "You've encountered this before?"

"Several times over the years. The first time it scared me pretty bad, though." He hesitated, then continued as he spread peanut butter onto a thick slice of bread. "I was on a dig in Tunisia with my dad and my stepmother. She got stung by a scorpion and had a terrible reaction to it. It took us six hours to get her to a doctor. She almost died."

Alicia shivered, despite the heat. "That must have been awful for you."

"It was worse for my dad. They'd only been married a couple of months, and Amy hadn't wanted to come on the dig at all, but Dad was committed and he talked her into it. The whole time during the trip to the hospital, he kept saying that if she died it would be his fault, that he'd killed her."

"She was all right, though, wasn't she?"

Dom nodded. "But you can bet that was the last dig she ever went on." The last for his father, as well, he added silently. That scorpion sting had put an end to the only way of life Dom had ever known. At age thirteen he was accustomed to traipsing around the world with Raymond, attending school wherever one could be found or relying on a tutor. After Tunisia, his family had settled in the small college town of Claymore, New York—Amy's home town—and hadn't budged.

The ensuing years were the worst in Dom's life. He'd never spent much time around kids his own age, and he'd had no common ground on which to base friendships in a small-town high school. He hadn't understood the other boys' passion for football, television or rock music. In turn, the kids he knew couldn't begin to relate to his former lifestyle. Isolation had fed his resentment toward both Amy and his father. It was only when he went away to college and started his formal training in archaeology that he was able to let go of the anger.

"Can't say I blame your stepmother for wanting to stay home," Alicia said casually. "If I had a scare like that, I wouldn't be eager to set foot outside my front door anytime soon."

And that was the rub, Dom thought with a sad ache in his chest. Women like Amy and Alicia—pretty, feminine and delicate—didn't belong in places like Tunisia, or here for that matter, with an uncivilized man like him. True, Alicia seemed to be tougher than she looked...but Amy had once seemed tough, too.

He stared down at the untouched bread and peanut butter. He didn't even like peanut butter.

"So, is it business as usual on Coconut Cay?" Alicia asked as she stood and drained the rest of her coffee. "We're minus two team members now."

"We'll manage," Dom replied dryly. "Today Skip can work with Ginny on Dog Tooth. You and Del will come with me to Mud Mound, at the south end of the island. After lunch I'll probably send you back to work in the lab."

"Or you could send Del back," Alicia suggested.

"I don't think you'll be so eager to stay at Mud Mound once you get a taste of it." He lifted one eyebrow and studied her again, taking in the white jeans that covered her slender legs, and a snug T-shirt with a wide neckline that emphasized the shadows and curves and smooth texture of her shoulders and neck. A tiny gold locket nestled just above the hollow between her breasts. She wore a different baseball cap today, a pink one that matched her shirt.

He looked forward to seeing those pristine clothes covered with mud. No volunteer he'd ever encountered managed to stay as cool and clean looking as she did. It made him wonder if she really did any work, or if she just made it appear that she did. But then he remembered the blisters on her soft hands. No, she couldn't have faked those.

After choking down the dry bread and peanut butter, Dom prepared his small party for the hike to Mud Mound. He instructed Del to slap together some cheese sandwiches and Alicia to mix orange juice from a bottled concentrate. Weighted down with these lunch rations, as well as various tools and other supplies, the party of three took off for the swamps.

Dom put his earlier, more dismal thoughts behind him as he led the way down the now familiar path toward Mud Mound, even managing a cheerful whistle. Alicia and Del followed, talking in quiet voices at first, then not at all as the way became more arduous, claiming all of their concentration.

To reach the recently discovered mound required wading through knee-deep water and climbing over and under tangles of mangrove roots and branches, then slogging through pools of ankle-deep mud—not an easy task, carrying fifteen or twenty pounds of awkward cargo. But even though Dom himself carried the heaviest load, he had to stop several times, waiting for his "team" to catch up.

"We're coming," Alicia called once after he'd stopped for the third time. "My legs aren't as long as yours and Del's. It's harder for me to climb over these roots."

Dom was undeniably disappointed in her. He'd thought she was above making excuses. And besides, he didn't think her legs were that much shorter than his. She had the proportions of a racehorse, despite her lack of height. Those legs were slender and firmly muscled, and earlier he had observed her moving with fluid agility.

"Could you slow down a little, Dom?" she called out again, a couple of minutes later. "I have to rest just a minute. My arms are about to fall off from carrying this cooler."

He stopped reluctantly and consulted his watch. They were already late getting to the mound. With a smaller team, they'd never finish the work he had scheduled for today— especially if one of his team members was wimping out on him.

"Your minute's up," he called over his shoulder. "Tough it out, Alicia. I thought you said you could handle the work."

"I can," she assured him. "But the second day's tougher than the first, you know? Sore muscles and all."

Something about her argument bothered him, but he wasn't sure what. It rang just a little bit insincere. Was it possible she was slowing him down on purpose, just to get his goat? He didn't think so. Alicia wasn't meek or passive, but neither was she malicious.

Maybe he ought to simply face the fact that she wasn't as tough as he'd come to believe—as strong as he'd hoped.

He ought to be grateful she was showing him the cracks in her armor. Her shortcomings made him feel . . . safer, somehow. Less susceptible to her allure, perhaps.

He'd flirted with a fatal mistake by kissing Alicia and by allowing himself to so openly want her. He was lucky she had more scruples about privacy than he did—damn lucky. He could never have made love to her casually, as he had other women. She had a way of getting to him, of sneaking dangerously close to his soul. If he'd accidentally allowed her too close, he might have been unable to let her go.

He stopped on a small, grassy rise, one of the few dry places in the vicinity. "This is it, folks," he announced.

Alicia dropped the cooler with a huff, then sat down on it. "Thank goodness." Her gaze took in the dead mangrove shoots, hundreds of twigs protruding from the mud. Even the live trees were no more appealing, for most of them were covered with the tiny land crabs that thrived all over the island. The hot, still air, the drone of insects and the oppressive odor of decay did nothing to improve the aesthetics of the swamp. "This place belongs in a horror movie," she said flatly. "Where's the mound?"

Dom pointed to a rectangular hole in the mud, about the size of an open grave, a few feet away from where they sat. It was filled almost to the brim with water. "Most of the site is below sea level," he explained. "The water seeped in last night, so we'll have to bail it out before we can dig." He patted her knee, leaving a small dirty smudge on the white denim. "Let's go."

She stood and brushed away the smudge, until she'd regained her pristineness. "I'm ready," she said, though she turned a worried glance toward Del.

"I'm ready," the older man echoed.

They set up a bucket brigade. Dom stood in the hole, immersed up to the thighs, and lifted out one bucketful after another of the murky water. He handed each one to Alicia, who then handed it to Del, who disposed of it a safe distance from the site.

Alicia was annoyingly inefficient, Dom thought as he watched her stagger slowly away from the excavation with the last bucket he'd passed to her. "Could you try to speed it up a little?" he sniped. "At this rate, the hole will fill up again before we can get it emptied."

"Maybe if you filled the buckets only halfway," Alicia suggested cheerfully, giving no indication that she resented his criticism. "My spirit is willing but my flesh—particularly the flesh on my arms—is weak."

Dom did as she asked, though he grumbled all the while. "A chain's only as strong as its weakest link," he muttered. Losing almost half his volunteer team was bad enough, but if the ones he had left couldn't put in a decent day's work, this digging season would be a bust. Of course, there would be another volunteer team after this one left, and then another. But once the dig was behind schedule, nothing short of a miracle would redeem it. If their efforts were further hampered by bad weather...he didn't even want to think about it. Grant money had a way of disappearing when no significant results were forthcoming.

"That's good enough," he said when only a few inches of water remained in the bottom of the excavation. "Alicia, you can start digging, and I'll show Del how to water screen. Later you can switch jobs."

"I have to get down there?" she asked, pointing into the deep hole. "How?"

"I'll help you," he said, offering her one muddy hand for support. "Just jump in." When she hesitated, he laughed. "You *aren't* planning to stay clean, are you?"

"Guess not." She took his hand gingerly in her gloved one, closed her eyes and made the plunge. Her impact sent muddy water flying in every direction—everywhere but on her. She looked down at herself, obviously pleased.

Dom rolled his eyes. The woman defied the laws of nature.

He showed Del and Alicia how to dig, using a trowel to shave thin layers of mud from a new square that had been measured off yesterday. Del watched from above as Alicia imitated Dom's technique. She picked it up quickly, and seemed genuinely pleased when she found her first pottery shard.

"This is a big one," she said, holding it up to examine it in the sunlight. "We didn't find anything this large yesterday, did we, Del? And look, isn't this part of the rim?"

"Very good," Dom said. "You're learning fast."

"Ginny explained to us how the rims are more valuable. Can you really tell what size and shape the pot was from this one piece?" Alicia asked, her speech animated.

Dom shrugged. "Won't know till I measure it. We'll probably find quite a few more like that before the day's out. This site is very well preserved and hasn't been looted like Dog Tooth Mound."

"Will we find any burials?" she asked excitedly.

Del made a face, indicating his distaste. "You're morbid, Alicia."

"Not here," Dom said with a grin. "This is a midden."

Alicia's navy blue eyes widened in surprise. "We're excavating a garbage dump?"

"That's right. You can learn a lot from analyzing refuse. Bones and shells tell us what these Mayan villagers ate, for instance."

"If you say so."

He looked at the pile of mud they had accumulated in the screen, and decided it was enough. With a fluidity of movement that came from years of practice, he climbed out of the hole without disturbing the delicate mud walls or the shelf that their digging had produced. "Grab one end of the screen," he instructed Del.

Awkwardly, they wrestled their load of mud to the water's edge. Then each of them found a mangrove root to perch on, and with the screen floating between them in the shallows, Dom showed the older man how to slosh it around in the water, then squeeze the mud with their fingers to find smaller artifacts that might have been missed.

Del took a deep breath. "Dom, I have to tell you something," he said. "Alicia's not the weak link in our chain, I am."

Dom looked up sharply. "What?"

"She wasn't slowing us down, I was. In fact, she was carrying her gear and half of mine most of the time, and helping me over the rough spots. And when we were bailing water, she deliberately slowed down the pace for my sake."

"Why would she do that?" Dom wanted to know.

"I threatened to go home yesterday. I have arthritis pretty bad, and I was afraid I'd make a fool of myself if I tried to keep up with all you young people. I knew this work would be too much for me. But Alicia didn't want me to leave. She promised to help me if I'd stay, and that's what she's been doing, this morning and all day yesterday, too, without letting anyone see. She's trying to save my pride. But I'm afraid it's at the expense of her own. I can't let her take the fall for me."

"I see." That's why her earlier complaints had rung so false in his ears, Dom realized. But he wouldn't think about her—not just yet. His concern now was Del. "I wish you'd told me about your arthritis. We can work around problems like that. Not all volunteers have the same abilities, and we certainly don't want to push you into doing more than you can handle. I'm perfectly willing to slow down the pace a little, or if you need to rest—"

Del's faded blue eyes took on a surprisingly hard glint. "You weren't willing to be that accommodating with Alicia."

Dom swallowed hard, then cleared his throat, refusing to meet the cold censure in Del's face. "I was a little hard on her," he admitted as he smashed another mud ball between his fingers. "I guess I just expected more from her, and she disappointed me." He'd begun to think she was special, different, maybe even a little extraordinary, and she'd crushed his hopes with her weakling act.

Silently they both examined what was left in the screen. They found only one small piece of chert, a rock that was remarkable only in the fact that it didn't occur naturally on Coconut Cay. Dom tucked it into a plastic bag.

"Alicia might not like it here," Del said, "but now that she's here, she'll give this job a hundred and ten percent of her effort. She never does anything halfway."

"Mmm-hmm," Dom responded, not quite ready to face a new assessment of Alicia.

"She'll do the work of two strong men, if you just give her a little encouragement and a word of praise now and then."

Dom stood abruptly. "I'll apologize to her, all right?" he asked impatiently. It seemed as if all he ever did was apologize to her. "I behaved like an ass, I can admit it."

Del's eyes, so cold only moments ago, twinkled now with amusement, but he made no reply.

"I'll go get another load of mud," Dom said, trudging back to shore, back toward Alicia.

He paused to study her from a distance. She was still working, her brow furrowed with concentration, and Dom felt his heart rise right into his throat. He was seeing her in a whole different light. She was a proud woman, and yet she'd sacrificed that pride for the sake of an old man. She *was* extraordinary, even more so than he'd previously suspected.

A sobering realization struck Dom. He'd thought he could survive these two weeks without getting tangled up with her as long as he maintained a safe physical distance. But even if they never made love, never even *touched,* he still wasn't safe. As long as she was anywhere within sight or hearing, he could feel her tugging on his emotions.

He wished there was a way to put more distance between them, but acting like a jerk wasn't the answer. She deserved better treatment than that, and if he gave her any less than she deserved, he'd never be able to look Del, or himself, in the eye.

Hell, he was already much too fond of her. How had it happened? He'd spent a lot of years holding people at a distance precisely so that he wouldn't have to deal with emotional attachments and their unpredictable results. Yet without even trying, this black-haired siren had excavated her way into his heart.

Five

Alicia ate two cheese sandwiches with the enthusiasm she normally reserved for filet mignon or a hot fudge sundae.

"And I always thought you were such a delicate thing," Del teased as he strapped on his backpack. "I've seen truckers eat with more refinement."

"This digging really works up an appetite," she replied happily as she opened the cooler, hoping to discover something else edible. She found an orange. "Are you, uh, sure you can find your way back okay?"

He smiled reassuringly. "No problem. I'll just follow the footprints most of the way." With that he took off for camp, using a sturdy walking stick he'd carved from a tree branch.

Alicia wasn't sure why Dom had changed his mind and sent Del back early instead of her, but she was glad he'd done it. Maybe Dom had noticed the older man's fatigue, but she hated to give the insensitive lout that much credit.

He certainly hadn't shown much compassion over her own fatigue, feigned though it was.

She stretched her legs out in front of her on the grassy hillock, then pulled her pocket knife out of her pack and began to peel the orange. Dom sat not three feet from her, because there wasn't any more room than that on the hill, finishing the last of the juice. They said nothing to each other for a while, but Alicia didn't mind the dearth of words. It was nice just to rest for a few minutes. A breeze had kicked up, dispersing some of the swamp's oppressiveness. That, combined with the sun, was making her drowsy.

"Would you really like to find a burial?" Dom asked after a while. "Some people are squeamish about that sort of thing."

"Not me," Alicia said. "I don't think the ancient Mayans would mind us picking their bones to learn about them—as long as we're not disrespectful about it. They were a scientific people, after all."

"I thought you said archaeology is a waste of time," he said casually.

She looked down, cringing inwardly at her own careless words thrown back at her. "I didn't really mean it. The pursuit of knowledge is never a waste of time. I just thought it was silly for someone like *me* to be mucking about in the dirt...."

"You still feel that way?" He looked at her intently, as if her answer really mattered.

"As filthy and exhausting as this work is, it does hold a certain appeal," she said cautiously. "I can see how someone would get addicted to it."

"*Addicted* is the right word," he said. "It gets in your blood."

"But I do feel out of place here," she added. "If you were to visit me where I work, you'd probably feel just as awkward."

He nodded, acknowledging the truth of her statement. "Alicia," he began slowly, "I find this hard to believe, but I owe you yet another apology."

She raised her eyebrows at him. "How many does this make, three?"

"At least. Anyway, I was rude and intolerant earlier, and I'm sorry. I know now you were just trying to help Del—"

"Don't let on to Del," she interrupted, alarmed to realize that Dom had seen through her ruse. "He's so worried that everyone will think he can't keep up—"

"Del's the one who told me," he said softly.

"Oh." She sighed. "He shouldn't have said anything. We were doing just fine."

"He couldn't stand it that you were taking the blame for his weakness," Dom said. "He's tremendously fond of you. I think he would have liked to pop me one right on the jaw for being impatient with you."

She looked at him sideways. "I had to curb that particular urge myself."

"Ah, hell, Alicia. I don't know what makes me say the things I do. Sooner or later everyone gets fed up with me—just ask Ginny and Renaldo. I can issue orders with no problem, but when it comes to dealing with people on a more personal level..." He shrugged helplessly. "I don't deal well with people."

She couldn't exactly disagree with him. He hadn't swept her off her feet with his witty repartee or his interpersonal skills. But he was basically a good person—that she knew. A little confused, maybe, but still good. The fact that he was trying to at least explain his behavior was a promising sign.

"Maybe you spend too much time in these isolated places," she ventured.

"Undoubtedly," he agreed. "But it's the only thing I know how to do, the only thing I'm good at."

"Somehow I doubt that," she said, then could have bitten her tongue out. The remark was undeniably suggestive and not at all what she'd wanted to convey—not consciously, at least.

If he caught it, he gave no indication. "Can I have some of that orange?"

"Sure." She split it open and handed him half.

The orange was sour and pulpy and seedy and tasted like heaven, Alicia thought as she allowed the juice to drip down her chin. The island seemed to enhance all of her senses. Colors looked brighter. She had become more aware of the subtlest odors, the faintest noises. Her fingertips had learned to discern the differences between an ordinary rock and a piece of pottery. She was more sensitive even to her own clothes and how they felt against her skin.

It was almost as if she were coming fully alive for the first time.

When she'd finished the orange, she wiped her mouth and chin with the bandanna tied around her neck, then heaved a deep sigh of satisfaction. "Is it time to get back to work?"

"Whenever you're ready," Dom replied as he wrapped up the debris from lunch and tucked it into the cooler.

They took turns digging and water screening, trading shifts every hour or so. But even then the work was agonizingly tedious, especially because they were finding virtually no artifacts, other than a few shells and some tiny pottery bits.

"Sometimes that's the way it goes," Dom said with a fatalistic shrug of his shoulders. "One square will yield all sorts of interesting things, while another next to it comes up dry."

"Nothing around here comes up dry," she said, looking down at her boots. She was immersed ankle-deep in the sticky mud, waiting for Dom to fill the screen so she could carry it to the water and sift.

"You want to switch?" he asked.

She yawned expansively. "No, I'll do one more screen-ful." She picked up the load of mud and slogged toward the water without much enthusiasm.

The tide was going out, she noticed as she picked her way through the mangroves. The root she'd been sitting on be-fore no longer offered a good enough access to the water. She waded out deeper, until she found another likely perch, then removed her gloves and proceeded to swish and slosh and mash the mud with her fingers, searching for elusive bits of the past.

She found several small shards this time, but nothing to cheer about. With a sigh of defeat she stood, picked up the screen and headed back toward the excavation. After only a few steps, however, she realized she'd taken a different route through the mangroves. Suddenly nothing looked fa-miliar.

"Great," she mumbled. All she needed was to get lost in the swamp. She paused, listening for the sound of the ocean and noting the direction of the sun, and soon she had her bearings again. She resumed her progress and had almost gained a firm footing on semidry land, when something just below the surface of the water snagged her foot. The screen flew out of her hands, along with the little artifacts, but she did manage to catch herself on a tree branch just in time to avoid plunging face-first into the muck.

"Damn, damn, *damn!*" she yelled when she'd recovered her footing. Although none of the pottery shards she'd lost were particularly significant by themselves, when lumped together they helped Dom to draw a picture of how the Ma-yan villagers lived—or how and where they dumped their trash, in this case. He wouldn't be too pleased that she'd scattered their finds all over the swamp.

"Alicia?" Dom called from the distance. "You okay?"

"Yes, I'm fine," she called back, silently cursing her own clumsiness. What had she tripped over, anyway? It had felt more substantial than a root—maybe a piece of boulder coral?

She felt around under the water with the toe of her boot until she located the offending object. Curious, she pulled off her gloves and plunged her hands into the muck, feeling her way across the thing's surface.

Her heart just about stopped. Boulder coral wasn't this smooth, this regular, and it didn't have handles.

"Dom!" she called excitedly. When he didn't answer her, she took off toward him, leaping over roots like a gazelle. After only a few steps she lurched to a stop and turned back, afraid she might not be able to find the spot again. She pulled off her bandanna and tied it around a nearby tree, then resumed her sloshing, forgetting the screen in her haste.

"It's about time," Dom said when he saw her emerge into the clearing. "Find anything?"

"Yes." She could hardly contain the excited laughter that threatened to bubble forth.

He stopped digging and gave her his full attention. "Well? What?"

"You'll have to come with me to see it. Come on, come on," she said when he hesitated.

Something about her manner quickened his pulse. Her face was flushed with excitement, and her eyes sparkled with mischief. Intrigued, he climbed out of the hole and followed her. He liked following her, he decided as he studied the way her white jeans clung snugly to the muscles of her lean hips and thighs. The jeans were still clean, too, he noted. Not one smudge marred the white denim. How did she do that?

She led him into a thick tangle of mangroves, a short distance from where they'd been screening. She stopped by one tree in particular, where she'd tied her scarf, then stooped down, beckoning him to do the same.

"Give me your hand," she said, and he willingly complied. She dragged his hand into the water with hers, then pressed his palm against something hard.

"Oh, my God," he said, finally understanding. He gently probed the object with both hands, letting his experienced fingertips tell him what his eyes couldn't. This was no schlock hunk of everyday pottery. This was a delicate piece of craftsmanship, with a satin-smooth surface and a finely etched design. There were no chips to mar the rim, at least not the part he could feel. A good portion of the pot was buried in swamp muck. But if he was lucky—and he had a good feeling about this one—the vessel would be intact.

Alicia looked on, waiting expectantly for his reaction. He could tell she wanted him to be pleased with her find, that she sought his approval, and that realization excited him almost more than the find itself.

"Well?" she demanded impatiently. "Isn't it neat? Do you think it's a whole pot? Can we dig it out? What do we do next?"

He grinned wickedly in answer, knowing exactly what he was going to do next. He scooped up two handfuls of slimy mud, then straightened purposefully.

"Well?" she said again, standing with him.

"It's a wonderful find, Alicia," he said, injecting a serious note into his voice. "It could be very significant. We'll know when we see the whole thing. But we can't dig it out until we've done a few other things, like photograph it and measure its coordinates and map it—"

She wrinkled her nose at him. "That sounds boring. I want to dig it out and take it back to camp to show everyone—I know, I know, an artifact is meaningless unless it's studied within a context. I've heard the lecture. So what *do* we do next?"

"We wait for the tide to go out, so we can see the thing and take pictures of it. And while we're waiting..." He eyed her immaculate clothing speculatively. "You're much too clean for anyone to take you seriously."

She saw the mud in his hands and instantly understood his intent. "Dom, no, that's not fair," she objected as she backed away. "I've worked really hard to stay clean—" She took another step back. "I find you a great pot, and this is how you thank me?" Her intended escape route was blocked by a tangle of roots. She stopped and stared defiantly up at him, knowing she was caught, daring him to do his worst.

Somehow she managed to look like a frightened doe and a fierce wildcat, all at the same time, and Dom was suddenly uninterested in mucking up her clothes. The game he'd started had taken on a decidedly dangerous overtone. He leaned forward menacingly, hands outstretched, but somehow it was his mouth instead of his hands that made the first contact.

All of Alicia's earlier excitement over the pot became fuel for the kiss; the wildcat part of her responded to him. While he was suddenly loath to soil her with his grimy hands, she pulled herself against him, apparently unconcerned with the state of her clothing. He gave in to the demands of the moment and wrapped his arms around her, knowing full well he was leaving muddy handprints on her back and her shapely little behind.

That was the last conscious thought he entertained for some time. He was lost in Alicia's kiss—not just in the feel of her demanding lips against his and her softness pressed to his hardness, but in the way she made him feel inside. For those few precious moments, he felt a bond with her, as if they shared the same consciousness. And for a brief, dizzying instant, he knew what it would feel like to love and be loved by a woman—by this woman. He had never, in his wildest imaginings, envisioned anything so euphoric.

Alicia could feel the squish of mud against her back, where Dom had pressed his hand against her. Oddly enough, the sensation was pleasant when combined with the warmth of his mouth against hers. She could still taste that sour orange they'd shared at lunch.

Good sense told her she should be offended over the way he had insinuated one of his legs between hers and the way he pressed his obvious arousal against her. She never would have tolerated such behavior back home. But his boldness seemed to suit him, and the situation, and she found that it only excited her further.

She could have wallowed in the mud and it would have only enhanced the feel of Dom's kiss. Why had she worried so much about staying clean? she wondered dazedly as his hands wandered around on her back, her hips and along her ribs, brushing the sides of her breasts. In a move that would have shocked her, had she been in her right mind, she took his hand and, much as she'd guided it to the submerged clay vessel a few minutes earlier, she guided it to her breast.

A low moan escaped from Dom's throat. "Alicia, what are you doing?" he rasped against her mouth. But he didn't resist her invitation and began to explore the contours of her breast with those knowing fingers.

"I . . . I don't know," she whispered back, finding speech difficult. "Re-responding, I think." Yes, definitely responding, she added silently, closing her eyes and tipping her head back as she fully appreciated the delightful sensations. Her nipples strained against the lace of her bra, causing her to wish wildly for the touch of Dom's hand against bare skin.

"I suppose I did start this," he said, dipping down to taste her neck. "But you can't blame me. It was just. . ." His voice trailed off as he paused to link a chain of kisses down her neck and across her collarbone, making her shiver despite the ninety-degree heat. "It was just the excitement of . . ."

"Finding the pot," she finished for him, eagerly latching on to the excuse he'd come up with. "All that adrenaline..."

"Adrenaline, right," he agreed.

She reached up to run her hand through his thick, unruly hair, then drew his face up to hers, eager to feel his mouth on hers again. He willingly obliged.

"Shouldn't we..." she said when she broke the kiss out of sheer overstimulation. If she didn't stop, she was going to flat-out faint.

"Shouldn't we what?" he muttered, transferring his attentions to her ear.

"Um, the pot. The afternoon's almost gone. Shouldn't we be doing something?"

Dom sighed as he gave her ear, and then her lips, a parting kiss. "You're entirely too right," he said, his voice full of obvious regret as he straightened her T-shirt. Still holding her loosely, he glanced over his shoulder at the site where she'd found the magnificent artifact. "Another five minutes or so," he said, gauging the progress of the receding tide with a practiced eye. "Meanwhile—"

He looked as if he might kiss her again, and she half hoped he would. But at the last moment he instead grasped her shoulders, held her at an arm's distance, and stared at her muddied clothes with mock surprise. "Why, Alicia, you're a mess!"

She laughed even as she leaned down to scoop up a handful of muddy ammunition. "Seems I owe you one," she said, taking a leisurely survey of his clothes, trying to decide where to strike. But everywhere she looked was already covered with mud. Furthermore, the sight of his mud-slick shirt molding itself to the hard planes of his torso caused another surge of awareness to wash over her. Good gravy, she'd just allowed a man to ravish her in a swamp... and had enjoyed it thoroughly.

She stopped smiling, and the mud fell harmlessly from her hand into the shallow water with a plop. "I'll go get the camera," she offered, suddenly uneasy with her recent behavior. She couldn't blame Dom entirely—she'd been a willing participant.

"It's in my backpack," he said, turning away from her, as if he, too, had cause to question what had just happened.

She quickly put some distance between them, slogging back to the hillock where their gear sat and using the time to sort out what was happening to her, to them.

Dom had indicated that he wanted to keep his distance and yet continually refused to do so. She'd told him in no uncertain terms that she didn't intend to become physically involved with him, and yet when he touched her she burned for him like a torch. If he'd asked her to, she would have lain down right there in the mud and made love to him.

Their attraction had taken on a life of its own, apart from what either of them wanted, apparently, and nothing they said or did seemed to dampen the desire, or keep it at bay. They'd lost control—what little they had to begin with. What really frightened her was not knowing what direction the raging fire inside her would take.

Of course there could be no future for them, she thought as she shouldered Dom's pack, nothing beyond the next few days. His place was here and hers was in Houston with her grandfather's company, hundreds of miles away. But that didn't mean there would be no repercussions. Whatever happened on this island could change her, forever. She could already feel herself changing inside, in small, subtle ways.

And on the outside, too, she mused with a rueful grin as she noted the state of her clothes.

By the time she returned to Dom, the pot was plainly visible above the waterline, shining with a pearlescent glow.

"It's beautiful, isn't it?" Dom said with a hushed reverence she'd never heard in his voice before.

"It is," she had to agree as she hung the backpack on a nearby tree and pulled out the 35 mm camera.

As she watched him photograph the vessel from every conceivable angle, Alicia began to understand the passion Dom held for his work. He could hardly take his eyes off the pot, he was so entranced with it. When he'd finished one roll of film and half of another, he finally decided he had enough shots.

"Now can we dig it out?" Alicia asked excitedly.

"First I have to take some measurements," he told her patiently, pulling a tape measure, string and pencil and paper from the backpack. "We don't even have any coordinates for this spot—we'll bring the transit here tomorrow and find out just where we are."

"You mean we have to leave it here until tomorrow?" she asked with an edge of despair.

"Well…" He considered the pot for a few moments. "It's in a pretty vulnerable spot and there's no way to protect it—"

"That's right! A storm could whisk it out to sea," she said, sounding almost happy over the prospect. "So let's dig it out."

"In good time." He took various measurements, plotted points on a piece of graph paper, and sketched in the main lines of the pot. Alicia looked over his shoulder with rapt attention, seemingly fascinated but also impatient. She was blocking his light and infringing on his elbow room, but he enjoyed her enthusiasm so much he didn't say anything.

When he was satisfied that he'd adequately recorded the vessel's position, Dom reached into his backpack once more and extracted his smallest trowel, which he reserved for delicate work. He handed it to Alicia. "It's your find. You get to unearth it."

"Really?" she squeaked. "But I couldn't . . . what if I do something wrong?"

"You'll do fine, and I'll be right here, coaching you. Just go slowly."

It turned out to be a delicate operation, accompanied by a lot of cursing and nail biting as each small bit of mud she removed revealed more and more of the pot. Finally, as the last of the daylight slipped away, the vessel was free. It was intact, just as they'd hoped, with only one small crack.

"Let's get out of here," Dom said after only a moment's celebration. He glanced around at the diminishing light with trepidation. "I just hope the batteries in my flashlight hold out."

Carrying only their essentials and leaving behind the rest, they made their slow way back to camp, using the flashlight sparingly to conserve the batteries. They lost their footing often, and the mangroves' wicked little branches seemed to reach out to snag clothing and hair. Alicia clung shamelessly to him, not for support but for reassurance, squeezing his arm more tightly at every strange noise. And he just as shamelessly enjoyed her small show of vulnerability. He knew she was strong and capable, but part of him liked to think that he could still protect her from nasty night-swamp things.

She loosened her grip only when the mangroves had given way to palm trees. "I was beginning to think my feet would never touch flat, dry ground again," she said, obviously relieved.

"Alicia . . ." He pulled her to a stop. "Before we rejoin the others . . . about what happened back there, I just want to say—"

"Don't you dare apologize again," she said sternly. "And don't ask me to forget it. That doesn't work."

"I wasn't going to do either," he said. "I just want to say that whatever it is I feel for you, it's not going away, and pretending it doesn't exist just makes me schizophrenic."

"So what do you suggest we do?" she queried, folding her arms. "Realistically, we just can't take it any further."

"I've never been a realist," he countered.

"We can't." She clenched her eyes closed. "I won't change my mind about this."

"Are you trying to convince me, or yourself?"

"Both of us. Look, Dom, this thing is already out of control. Let's rein it in while we have the chance."

"We tried that."

"Then we'll have to try harder. This might be just a fling for you, but I'm not going back home with my head messed up and my heart in pieces." She turned away and started off ahead of him.

"Alicia." The single clipped word brought her to a halt. "That's not a fair assessment. From the very beginning, it's been more than a physical thing on my part. You know that. Dammit, you *know* that. You're the one who pointed it out to me."

"Yes," she said, still not facing him.

"Then why—"

"Because it's what I want to believe. Because it would be much easier to turn my back on you if I can believe you don't really care."

"But I do care. And so do you, I think. And it's too late to pretend otherwise. Regardless of what happens, when you leave I'm going to miss you. My mind's already messed up and my heart—well, I'm not sure what's going on there."

There was a long pause before Alicia spoke. "I'll think about what you've said. I can't promise any more than that."

"Fair enough."

The moon had risen, illuminating the path enough that Alicia could find her way back to camp without his aid. He let her walk on ahead of him.

Had his father gone through this with Amy? he wondered. Had Raymond tried to fight his attraction to her and failed? Maybe he'd had no more control over his feelings than Dom had right now.

At least neither he nor Alicia were crazy enough to try to make this thing work on a long-term basis. She'd said it herself—she felt awkward here. She belonged back in Houston, with her high-rise corporate office and her silk suits and her weekly manicures, designing office products of the future. And he belonged here, close to the earth, immersed in the past.

There was no way he'd ever leave his fieldwork behind. Years ago he'd vowed never to let anyone or anything force him to live in the present-tense, fast-paced real world again. That conviction was every bit as strong now as it ever had been.

Dinner was a strained affair. Ginny was irritated with Dom for staying out in the swamp so late and worrying her silly, and even the impressive sight of the Mayan vessel hadn't nudged her out of her stubborn temper.

Skip, too, had been out of sorts, downright quarrelsome, even. Apparently Ginny had put him to work for several hours in the "lab"—the front porch, the only part of the old house that had sound flooring. Cleaning, sorting, weighing and labeling artifacts was not the sort of work that agreed with him. Neither had he enjoyed cooking dinner, even though he was the one who had emphasized that they should all take turns with domestic duties, in the spirit of cooperation.

The fact that Alicia had turned up such an exciting find by sheer accident had only irritated Skip further. Whether he admitted it or not, he was competing with his cousin, perhaps because he actually believed that Eddie J. was testing them, Alicia mused.

Del was disturbingly quiet, causing Alicia to worry that life on Coconut Cay was still too hard on him, even with the concessions she and Dom had made.

Renaldo had not returned from the mainland after taking Robert to the doctor, so Alicia couldn't rely on his colorful stories to entertain her.

The only person left in a reasonably good humor was Dom, and she didn't want to spend any more time with him at the moment, not when there was such a delicate matter still dangling between them.

So Alicia had found a secluded spot in which to eat her fish, beans and rice—which were tasting better all the time. Then, after washing a few dishes, she'd pleaded a headache and gone to bed early, grimy and exhausted.

Some time before dawn the crab disturbed her sleep once again, scritch-scratching against the nylon right by her ear. The pesky crustacean had excavated a network of tunnels all about her tent, ruining the neat rain trench Dom had dug around the perimeter. She'd tripped over one hole and dropped her flashlight down another. Catching the beast and eating him was gaining appeal all the time.

It was still at least an hour before dawn, but Alicia knew she wouldn't be able to go back to sleep. She was wide awake now and surprisingly refreshed—but still gritty feeling. A bath was definitely in order.

She pulled on her swimsuit and an old pair of tennis shoes, then grabbed soap, shampoo and a beach towel. Ginny had told her about a secluded cove not far from camp, perfect for bathing, and Alicia intended to find it.

As she made her way along yet another path forged through the jungle, she was surprised that she didn't need her flashlight. The moon had long since disappeared, but the faint starlight was adequate. A couple of days ago she never would have contemplated running around in a strange part of the jungle at night, alone, much less without a flashlight. But a lot of things that had been foreign and frightening upon her arrival now seemed normal.

She found the cove exactly where Ginny had said it would be, and for a moment Alicia just paused to admire it. The sea, capable of producing the violent, crashing waves that had made her seasick, now lapped gently against the narrow strip of sandy beach. The water was so dark and calm that she could see the faint reflections of the tall palms that stood sentinal over the cove.

She draped her towel over a fallen tree, then waded eagerly into the welcoming water. It caressed her skin with a delicious freshness, inching cool fingers up her thighs, her hips, her middle and finally her breasts and shoulders as she submerged herself up to the neck.

With a laugh of sheer delight she dunked her head, then shampooed her hair and soaped her body, scrubbing until she felt clean—really clean—for the first time in three days.

Something made her think of Dom—maybe it was the feel of her own hands against her skin—and she wished she could share this place and this wonderful experience with him. She'd known him such a short time, and yet thoughts of him were becoming as normal as breathing—and almost as essential. She knew with utter certainty that he was capable of stirring up indescribable pleasures within her body. But it wasn't just the physical that tempted her. He could stir her emotions, too, to heights she'd never dreamed of.

She might never feel this way about anyone again. But a full-blown affair with Dominic Seeger would have its drawbacks. If she gave in to her desires, their inevitable parting would be that much more painful—and her memories bittersweet. But if she continued to fight nature, she would wonder for the rest of her life about the sweet ecstasy that might have been.

She drifted on her back for a while, staring up at the brightening sky, still with no answers.

Dom found her like that, floating serenely as if held by unseen hands. Her skin glowed in the dawn light with an energy all its own, and he paused for a few seconds just to admire the fetching sight she presented.

But only a few seconds. He didn't have any more than that.

"Alicia!" he called to her. Her head snapped to attention, and he motioned urgently for her to come to shore.

When she gained the beach, he held her towel for her. Instead of handing it to her, he wrapped it around her shivering body, holding her close for one instant before releasing her. He wished like hell he didn't have to destroy her morning calm.

"What's wrong?" she asked, looking up at him with large, fearful eyes as she absently blotted water droplets from her skin.

"It's Del. He's having chest pains. I'm taking him to the clinic on the mainland myself, and I need you to come with us."

Six

Alicia threw on the first T-shirt she could put her hands on, then a wrinkled pair of walking shorts, knee socks and her tennis shoes. She grabbed her day pack and flew out of the tent, taking off at a dead sprint. But even though her preparations had taken her less than two minutes, the boat was waiting for her.

She clamored on board, wrestling with the life jacket and rain poncho Ginny had thrust into her hands. Before she could even find a seat, Dom started the outboard and Skip was pushing the dory into deeper water.

"Sit in front," Dom yelled over the motor's roar.

She complied, but she sat facing toward the back where she could keep an eye on Del. He was stretched out on the bottom of the boat, leaning back against his bedroll and duffel bag. He was pale, and his face glistened with perspiration. Alicia had hoped the sight of him would quell her panic, that he wasn't as bad off as she'd feared, but she was disappointed.

He opened his eyes, focused on Alicia and awarded her a watery smile. She gave him a "thumbs-up" before his eyelids drifted closed again.

As the dory tipped from side to side, picking up speed, Alicia was reminded uncomfortably of the last time she'd ridden in such a boat. Renaldo's dory was bigger than this little dugout and more stable, too. Yet riding in it had caused a case of motion sickness for the record books. She wondered if she was about to give a repeat performance. If she became ill, Dom would have two invalids on his hands instead of one.

She absolutely could not allow that to happen, even if she had to stave off seasickness by sheer force of will.

She spared a glance toward Dominic. He sat in the stern, guiding their craft with an expert hand on the motor. His darkly tanned face was a study in grim determination as he surveyed the waters ahead of them.

He looked the perfect pirate, she thought, with the wind running wild fingers through his thick hair. The beard stubble that shadowed his chin, and the white shirt that billowed and snapped in the wind, only added to the illusion. If he'd come from another time, he probably would have been an adventurer, captaining one of those romantic sailing ships.

Perhaps he'd simply been born in the wrong century, she thought with a peculiar sadness in her heart, and that was why the past held such a fascination for him. He seldom spoke of any experiences other than those connected with his archaeology. She had a sneaking suspicion that those long-dead Mayans would hold his interest a lot longer than a present-day city girl like her.

The errant thought surprised her. Just exactly how long did she plan to hold his interest?

He caught her eye then, and the harsh lines of his face softened immeasurably. He was a passionate man, but he was also capable of tenderness. She'd seen that this morning, when he'd wrapped her towel around her shoulders as if she were made of fragile crystal.

About an hour into the crossing, Dom slowed the motor to idling speed. Alicia shot him a questioning look.

"I'm calling ahead to the marina," he explained as he pulled a hand-held radio from a plastic bag under his seat. "We're only just now within range. I'll see if they can have the taxi waiting for us."

"*The* taxi?" Alicia asked.

He smiled crookedly. "Punta Blanca only has one—when the owner's not too drunk to drive it, that is."

While Dom made his call, she took advantage of the momentary stillness to check on Del. She knelt beside him and took his hand; he opened his eyes once more.

"How're you doing?" she asked, trying to sound cheerful.

"'Bout the same," he confided. "My chest hurts like hell. But I'm still kicking."

"You'll be fine," she said as she offered him a sip of water from her canteen. "You've never had heart problems before, have you?"

He shook his head. "My doctor checked me out for this trip. Said the old ticker was sound as a Japanese yen." But Del's breathing was rapid and labored, Alicia noticed. She tried to remember everything she knew of first aid, but her mind was a blank. If his condition worsened before they reached the village clinic she'd be useless.

Dom finished his call and signaled for Alicia to resume her seat, and soon they were once again under way. The sun crept its way higher into the sky, and after a few minutes the heat was stifling. Her stomach started to roll with the boat.

When next she looked up at Dom, he was staring at her with marked concern. "Are you sick?" he called. The wind whipped away his words, but she could read his lips.

She shook her head, determined not to let her discomfort show. Eddie J. had taught her to bear hardship with stoicism. All of her attention as well as Dom's needed to be focused on getting Del into a doctor's care.

"Turn around!" Dom called out. "Face forward and keep your eyes on the horizon."

She did as he instructed, surprised that after a few minutes of feeling the wind in her face, her queasiness subsided. She spared a glance over her shoulder every so often to check on Del—and to catch a glimpse of Dom in his pirate pose—but the rest of the time she kept her eyes on the village ahead of them, which grew larger with every passing minute.

An hour later they were docking at the shabby marina, which was nothing more than a crumbling stone pier and one lone gas pump. A skinny boy tied up the boat, scampering barefoot over the rocks like a monkey. He was probably no older than six or seven, Alicia guessed, but he was stronger than he looked. He helped them get Del out of the boat and into the back seat of the rusty taxi that awaited them.

Alicia climbed into the back with Del and took his hand in hers. "Any better?" she asked anxiously.

"No better, no worse," he answered, giving her hand a weak squeeze.

As soon as Dom had jumped into the front seat, the elderly driver roused himself from his nap and navigated the car toward the clinic. The booming metropolis of Punta Blanca encompassed perhaps twenty square blocks, Alicia had figured the first time she'd seen it, the day of her arrival in Belize. The clinic couldn't be too far. But dogs, chickens and children clogged the streets, slowing their progress.

"Market day," the driver explained. The ride to the clinic took a slow five minutes.

By some miracle of communication, the clinic's young doctor had learned of their impending arrival and was prepared for them. He and his lone nurse, a wizened little nun, put Del in a wheelchair and whisked him away with an efficiency that surprised Alicia, given the agonizingly slow pace shown by the rest of the village.

There was no admitting desk, no forms to fill out—nothing to keep Alicia and Dom busy. There was just a small waiting room with an odd assortment of chairs and an ancient oscillating fan to stir the hot, humid air.

Alicia sank into one of the chairs, weak with anxiety, while Dom paced.

"Are you feeling all right?" he asked suddenly. "You looked a little green a while ago, on the boat."

She waved away his concern. "I'm better now."

"Let's stop and get you some motion sickness pills before we head back."

"Yes, fine," she said absently. Seasickness was the least of her worries right now.

Dom paced some more. "How about something cold to drink? There's a little store across the street."

"How can you think about cold drinks at a time like this?" she exploded, springing out of her chair. "Del might be dying!"

Dom's eyes widened, and he took her shoulders in a firm grip. "Calm down," he said sternly before releasing her. "I know Del is sick, but I'm a little worried about you, too. You didn't get any breakfast and you don't look so hot."

"What's wrong with the way I look?" she wanted to know.

"For starters, your shirt's on inside out, your socks don't match, and one shoe is untied. That's rather careless for a woman who can spend a whole day in a swamp, wearing *white,* and not get even a smudge on her."

"Oh." As she ran a hand through her wind-snarled hair, which she hadn't even combed after her swim, she conceded Dom the point. "I dressed in a hurry," she mumbled, searching for a comb in the day pack strapped around her waist. When she found it, she walked to the open doorway and stared unseeing into the dirt street as she began to work the tangles out of her hair.

She felt him come up behind her, and she didn't protest when he took the comb from her hand and began working out the snarls himself, with infinite gentleness.

"I've never seen hair as black and shiny as yours," he said softly.

"It's my Irish blood," she said, wondering why he was being so patient with her, after the way she'd lit into him. "My mother was named O'Dwyer."

"Is that where you got your temper, as well?" he teased.

"Um, yeah, about my temper—sorry I lost it there for a minute. It's not you I'm angry with." She turned to face him, knowing she had to put the awful truth into words. "Del wanted to go home two days ago and I wouldn't let him. Now here we are, hours away from any hospital, and he might be having a heart attack. If anything happens to him—" She swallowed hard and bit down on her knuckle to keep the tears at bay.

"Oh, Alicia, don't," Dom said as he wrapped his arms around her protectively. "Don't blame yourself. You had no way of knowing this would happen."

There was no passion in his embrace this time, just security and comfort, which she accepted without question. Right now she needed both. She'd never felt so wretched.

Dom held her silently for a long time, reminded once again of how small and delicate she was. He could probably crush her if he squeezed too hard. He felt like a heel for being so tough on her at Mud Mound. How could he have dumped all that backbreaking work on such fragile shoulders? All he wanted to do now was protect her and absorb her pain.

After a few minutes she struggled out of his grasp and turned away again, seemingly embarrassed over her emotional outburst.

He touched her hair lightly. "I know you're scared," he said. "It's all right to show it."

They said nothing for a while, both staring out into the street. A small girl, her broad face and wide-set eyes testimony to her Mayan heritage, ran past them chasing a skinny rooster. Her cry of gleeful triumph when she caught the squawking bird made both Dom and Alicia laugh briefly before lapsing back into silence.

After a few minutes Alicia took a deep breath and turned to look at Dom, her expression earnest. "Yesterday you said you weren't good with people. You don't give yourself enough credit. You're good with me. You've said and done all the right things today." She squared her shoulders. "I'm glad I don't have to go through this alone."

Now it was his turn to be embarrassed, he thought as he mumbled something noncommittal. But he took her words to heart. He was glad he could be of some comfort to her. And she was right. He did find it easier to talk to her than he did most other women. Maybe he didn't always say the right things, but the channels of communication were there.

The door to the inner office opened, grabbing Dom's attention. The tall, thin doctor neither smiled nor frowned, but there was a merry twinkle in his eyes that told Dom more than words could have.

Four Silhouette Special Editions FREE! *Plus*

APPLY TODAY AND WE'LL ALSO SEND YOU THIS CUDDLY TEDDY FREE!

Special Editions bring you all the heartbreak and ecstasy of involving and often complex relationships as they unfold today. And to introduce to you this powerful, contemporary series we'll send you four Special Edition romances, a cuddly teddy bear **PLUS** a mystery gift absolutely **FREE** when you complete and return this card.

We'll also reserve a subscription for you to our Reader Service, which means that you'll enjoy:

▶ **Six wonderful novels** - sent direct to you every month.
▶ **Free postage and packing** - we pay all the extras.
▶ **Free monthly Newsletter** - packed with competitions, author news and much more.
▶ **Special offers** - selected only for our subscribers.

Claim your **FREE** gifts overleaf

FREE BOOKS CERTIFICATE

Yes Please send me four **FREE** Silhouette Special Editions together with my **FREE** gifts. Please also reserve a special Reader Service subscription for me. If I decide to subscribe, I shall receive six superb new titles every month for just £10.50 postage and packing **FREE**. If I decide not to subscribe I shall write to you within 10 days. The free books and gifts will be mine to keep in any case. I understand that I am under no obligation whatsoever - I may cancel or suspend my subscription at any time simply by writing to you.

NAME _____

ADDRESS _____

_____

_____

POSTCODE _____

SIGNATURE _____

I am over 18 years of age.   **9S2SE**

Offer expires 31st December 1992. The right is reserved to change the terms of this offer or refuse an application. Readers overseas and in Eire please send for details. Southern Africa write to Book Services International Ltd., P.O. Box 41654, Craighall, Transvaal 2024. You may be mailed with offers from other reputable companies as a result of this application. If you would prefer not to share in this opportunity please tick box. ☐

A MYSTERY GIFT POST TODAY!

We all love mysteries - so as well as the FREE books and cuddly teddy, we've an intriguing FREE gift for you.

No stamp needed

Reader Service
FREEPOST
P.O. Box 236
Croydon
CR9 9EL

"Your friend is not having a heart attack," the doctor said in a thick patois that Dom still had trouble understanding, though he'd spent a lot of time among the native Belizians. "His pain is caused by muscle spasms, no doubt brought on by stress."

Alicia sighed with unabashed relief. "Then he'll be all right?"

The doctor nodded. "I've given him a muscle relaxant and a mild tranquilizer. But I think he should not go back to the island. There is too much risk for one his age who is unaccustomed to the work."

Dom concurred with that opinion. He wondered if Del would agree.

The doctor grinned then, and punched Dom playfully on the shoulder. "Your expedition has provided me with plenty of work this week, yes? First there was the burn, then the allergy and now this. Tomorrow you'll bring me a broken leg—or do you have anyone left to dig?"

Dom smiled back. "I'm down to two. One of those, at least, I couldn't get rid of even if I wanted to. She could break her leg and still be out there digging."

He shot a sideways look at Alicia, to see how she was handling his teasing. But her attention was focused on the door behind the doctor, where Del had just appeared. He waved away the elderly nurse's assistance.

"Del!" Alicia launched herself at him and threw her arms around his neck. "I'm so glad you're okay. How do you feel?"

"Jeez, Alicia, stop embarrassing me," he said gruffly, disengaging himself from her enthusiastic embrace. "It's bad enough everyone made so much fuss over some lousy muscle spasms."

He looked much better already, Dom noted. His color was more normal now, at least. Dom glanced uneasily at his watch, wondering how he should broach the subject of sending Del back to Houston. Fortunately he didn't have to apply any pressure. Alicia did it for him.

"You scared us half to death, you know," she said to the older man after he'd paid the doctor's modest bill. "We're putting you on the first plane out of here, and I don't want to hear any arguments."

"Me, argue?" Del responded. "If there's not a plane leaving in the next half hour, I'll *walk* back home." He turned to Dom. "No offense, but I'd rather face a firing squad than go back to that island of yours."

"No offense taken," Dom said mildly. "And you don't have to walk. There should be a plane leaving for Belize City at eleven. If you can make a connection there, you'll be home in time for dinner."

"Thank God. I can already taste my wife's pot roast," Del said dreamily as they left the clinic. He paused getting into the taxi and cast a meaningful glance at Alicia. "And I don't give a damn what Eddie J. says. This whole trip was a harebrained scheme. We should have gone to a golf resort, like Skip wanted to do in the first place."

Alicia reluctantly agreed. "Not one of Eddie's more inspired ideas. A resort would have caused less wear and tear on the staff. But you know Eddie J.—he doesn't believe in doing anything the easy way."

Within an hour she and Dom were standing at the airstrip, watching as the small prop plane took off bearing Del back to civilization. When it had veered out of sight. Alicia gave a resigned shrug and turned to Dom.

"Guess that's that. I'll miss him, but I'll sleep better knowing he's home safe."

"Me, too," Dom said.

"Hey, how about that cold drink you offered earlier?"

"I'll do you one better, I'll buy you lunch. There's a great little café near the marina that serves the most incredible fish—"

Alicia scowled.

"Would you prefer a greasy cheeseburger and French fries?" he tried again.

Her frown transformed itself into a glowing smile. "Now you're talking!"

Their taxi had disappeared, so they walked the few blocks back to the waterfront, to the café Dom had described. "It's not much to look at," he said, seeing the place through Alicia's eyes. The curtains were torn, the windows dirty, the tile floor cracked and uneven. "But the food's good, I promise."

"I don't care *what* it looks like," Alicia said gamely, zeroing in on the cleanest-looking table. "I'd kill for a decent burger, and this beats sitting on a bucket under that decrepit house, eating fish and fighting the smoke from the campfire."

"Why, Alicia, that sounds suspiciously like a complaint," he said as he took the seat across from her, signaling for the waitress to bring beer. "Don't you care for Coconut Cay's mealtime ambiance?"

She covered her face in mock chagrin. "Please forgive me. I didn't mean to malign your lovely island. But for a moment I was overwhelmed by all these big-city trappings. Do you know that they have a real bathroom at the airport? With running water and everything? It's gone to my head."

Before Dom could think of a suitably smart comeback the waitress arrived with two frosty mugs of beer. Alicia smiled sweetly at her and, without blinking, ordered a double hamburger with everything, as well as French fries *and* onion rings.

Dom placed a somewhat more conservative order, then sipped his beer and gazed out the window, relaxing for the first time that day. When he turned his attention toward Alicia, though, she didn't appear to share his frame of mind, despite her seeming good humor. She worried her lower lip with her teeth, and a small furrow between her eyebrows marred her smooth forehead.

"So, tell me about your life in Houston," he said, attempting to draw her out. "Have you always been involved in office products?"

She nodded. "I've worked for the company since I was sixteen. It's what I always wanted to do—work with my grandfather. A lot of people push their children into joining the family business, but it was never like that with me."

"You must really enjoy your work."

"Some parts of it," she agreed. "Now that I'm in management, I don't get to do as much of the actual design work as I like, and the corporate red tape drives me crazy, but . . . yes, I like it."

He caught the slight hesitation in her answer and wondered what it meant. She didn't sound a hundred percent sincere. "Are your parents involved with the business, also?" he asked.

Before answering she took a sip of the icy beer the waitress had brought. "No. They're divorced. My father worked at Bernard for a while, when I was a baby, but now he lives in Reno. He's in the hotel business. I haven't seen much of him over the years, not since I was a kid. I think that's why my grandfather took such a keen interest in me. He thought I needed a father figure."

"And your mother?"

"She lives in Houston, has a bookkeeping business. She's planning to retire in a couple of years."

"Brothers and sisters?"

"Nope. Just good ol' cousin Skip."

"Ah, yes, Skip." Dom tried not to show his distaste at the mention of her twerpy cousin. "You know, he was real put out that Del wanted you to come with us to the mainland instead of him."

Alicia laughed. "I think Skip is looking for any legitimate excuse to get off that island. Archaeology just doesn't agree with him. He has no patience."

"That's an understatement. He suggested we go at Mud Mound with shovels. Then he wondered why I didn't just bring a backhoe to the island."

"Still, you can bet he won't give up, not unless I do," Alicia said. "There's always been a sort of sibling rivalry between us. He wouldn't be able to stand it if I outlasted him."

"Is that why you're so determined to stay on?" Dom asked. "Because you don't want your cousin to outshine you?"

Apparently she took offense at that, for her eyes went to an even darker shade of blue and her finely arched brows drew together menacingly. She leaned forward until her face was inches from his. "I want to stay on because I agreed to do a job, and I'll do it if it kills me."

"Are you always so determined?" he asked, amused and intrigued by her show of wildcat fierceness.

"I didn't earn a vice presidency at Bernard Office Products by backing down," she replied tartly, settling back in her chair. "Some people think my grandfather gave me a cush job with a fat salary because I'm family. But that's not how Eddie J. operates. If anything, I had to work harder to prove myself to him, because I *am* his granddaughter. It was a tough decision, when he gave me that last promotion."

"And you figure that if you give up and go home early, he might question his judgment?"

"Why can't you just accept the fact that I honor my obligations?" she said with a sharp bang of her fist on the tabletop.

"Don't get all bent out of shape," he said, for he really hadn't intended to rile her up. "Maybe I'm being blunt, but I never claimed to have much tact. Anyway, all I'm trying to do is understand why you're so persistent. Now that more than half your team is gone, you can't possibly meet your original objective. You and your co-workers can't learn to work better together if most of them are gone. So why are you still here? It can't be because you're enjoying yourself."

He waited, holding his breath. Her answer was suddenly significant.

She studied him thoughtfully for a moment. "All right. Maybe I *am* trying to impress my grandfather. But you'd have to know Eddie J. to understand why. When I was a kid I lived for a word of praise from him. He's a good man, one I respect, and when he's proud of me, it means something."

"And that's all you're looking for?" Dom asked. "Just a nod of approval?"

She paused to think about her answer as the waitress put their food on the table. "When he chooses his successor, his decision won't be based on what happens here in Belize. But even if I thought he was testing us, I don't want to take over the company. Ever," she said as she dumped a healthy dollop of ketchup over her fries.

The vehemence behind her answer gave him food for thought. She wasn't your typical corporate executive, aiming for that next rung on the ladder. In fact, he got the distinct impression that she'd already climbed higher than she wanted to be.

They ate in silence for a while. Dom watched Alicia as she devoured her burger with obvious relish, closing her eyes from time to time to savor the treat. In the short time he'd known her, he'd never seen her look quite so sublimely satisfied—not even when he'd fed her chocolate. He found himself wishing he were responsible for the expression on her face.

"There's something else," she said when she'd nearly cleaned her plate. "I *am* enjoying myself. So there."

"You gotta be kidding."

"Look at the way I just inhaled that hamburger. I'd never eat like that at home. Something about this place makes me . . . live harder. You were right about the adjustment being difficult, but now that I've been here a couple of days, it's kind of growing on me.

"And yesterday," she continued, her eyes sparkling with enthusiasm, "when I found that pot—no feeling has ever equaled that, not even when I saw my first design roll off the assembly line. There's a real challenge to surviving here, and meeting that challenge is satisfying in a way I never dreamed possible."

She stopped herself self-consciously, as if she thought she'd said too much. "I don't know why I'm explaining it to you. You must know exactly what I'm talking about."

"Exactly," he managed, trying not to show the effect her words had on him. But he couldn't help the goofy smile that overtook his lips. Hope was virtually blooming inside him. Maybe she *could* adapt to his world. It was a long shot, against nearly impossible odds. But he knew now that he had to pursue that slim chance.

The east wind was definitely brisker by the time they returned to the dory. Dom had stopped to buy a few essentials, like beer and chocolate bars, which he stowed under the bow and strapped in tightly.

"We sure don't want to lose that chocolate," Alicia said with exaggerated solemnity. She was in a much better mood now that her stomach was full. She felt silly for having snapped at Dom—not once, but twice. She could have blamed her behavior on stress, but she was a corporate executive—she was supposed to be able to handle stress without losing her temper.

She had to give Dom credit for taking her bad humor in stride. He'd been a real sport today. She would have thanked him for being so tolerant, but she just didn't know how to begin.

They were fifteen minutes from shore when Dom abruptly turned the boat around.

Alicia whirled to face him. "What are you doing?"

"We forgot the—" She couldn't catch the rest.

"What?"

He slowed the boat to idling speed. "We forgot the motion sickness pills."

"We can't go back now," she objected. "I'll be okay. Coming over wasn't too bad."

"But the water is a lot rougher now. The wind's picked up." He worriedly eyed a bank of dark gray clouds on the horizon.

"We'll never beat that storm if we don't keep going," she reasoned. "Don't worry about me. Even if I do get sick, I'll be fine as soon as I get to dry land."

He looked at her doubtfully, then closed his eyes and nodded. "All right. I'll stay in close to the chain of islands, though, instead of heading for open sea. It might take a little longer, but the trip should be smoother."

"Whatever you think," she said, forcing more optimism into her voice than she felt. A few minutes late she had reason to doubt his decision. The boat pitched and rocked, scooting alarmingly close to the sharp coral heads that protruded from the water. If this was "smoother," she'd hate to see rough. She was soaked with the salt spray and shivering—the approaching storm had obliterated the sun, so hot only minutes earlier.

One glance at Dom's worried face told her he, too, regretted his decision.

"Let's head for open water!" she called to him, pointing for emphasis. "It can't be any worse than this!"

He fixed his gaze on the distant horizon, then shook his head. "It's too rough. We'd be swamped."

Better that than to be dashed to bits on the rocks, she wanted to say. But when she again assessed the open water, she changed her mind. The whitecaps looked larger and more numerous than they had only minutes ago, and they pounded thunderously against each other.

"I'm heading to shelter," she heard him say.

She nodded, relieved. If they were forced to ride out the storm, she'd rather do it with her feet firmly planted on the ground than at the mercy of the unpredictable sea.

But her relief lasted only seconds. As Dom turned the boat toward the closest island, a tiny, uninhabited cay, she heard a sickening crack, then felt a violent lurch. The outboard motor bucked hard, then seemed to jump right off the back of the boat.

Dom's reflexive lunge toward the motor only worsened the situation. As if in slow motion, the dory tipped to one side, hovered there for a moment, then turned belly up, plunging its occupants and cargo into the churning water.

Seven

Alicia's life jacket pulled her to the surface like a cork—but not before she'd inhaled half a gallon of salt water. Coughing and choking, and hampered by her clothing and the pack strapped to her waist, she tried to swim toward the overturned boat, a distressing distance away. Each time she thought she was making headway another wave would swamp her, negating her progress.

She spit out yet another mouthful of water. "Dom?" she called out. But she couldn't see him anywhere. That's when she felt panic closing in around her.

"Oh, God, no," she sobbed, then once again attempted to reach the boat. She kicked like a demon, losing one of her tennis shoes in the process. The waves pushed her against an outcropping of rock. She grabbed on to it, then frantically searched again for Dom. She still couldn't find him.

How could he leave her like this, to drown alone? Knowing that her own efforts were all she had to save her, she kept hysteria at bay. With a final burst of energy she pushed off from the rock and swam with all her might toward the boat, which had lodged against some coral. By some miracle, the previously uncooperative sea pushed her in the right direction this time. She reached out to grab one edge of the boat, then clung to it with a death grip as the fickle waves tried to pull her away again.

"Hold on tight!" a voice behind her cautioned.

She swung her head around, almost sick with relief when she saw that Dominic was right at her shoulder. She wanted to throw her arms around him and reassure herself that he was real and unharmed, but he didn't give her the chance.

"We've got to get the boat flipped over and away from this coral head," he told her, "or the waves will pound it into kindling." Even as he spoke he was climbing up onto the slippery coral.

Alicia again pushed her fear aside. Their survival depended on her actions at this moment. With cool detachment, she followed his instructions for righting the dory.

She pulled from one side as he pushed from the other, and their leverage tipped the dory right side up. Within seconds Dom had climbed aboard, but all Alicia could do was cling to the gunwales and drift with the boat. She had used up her last reserves of strength. Now her muscles felt about as substantial as the overcooked rice she'd had for dinner the night before.

"Get in," he ordered.

She groaned in protest, but he didn't hear her. With his typical no-nonsense attitude, he was hanging over the back of the boat, pulling on something. Seeing that he didn't intend to help her, she swung one leg over the side and more or less clawed her way aboard.

"Watch it! You're about to tip us over again," Dom cautioned sharply as he kept his attention focused on his task. "Alicia, I need help."

And I need a new pair of lungs, she longed to retort, but she didn't have the energy. She sat listlessly in the bottom of the boat, trying to catch her breath.

"Alicia," Dom called again. "Hurry up, this thing weighs a ton."

"Yes, I'm coming," she finally managed as she crawled toward him, not daring to stand in the violently rocking dory. When she was close enough, he could see that he had a firm grip on the outboard motor, but was having trouble pulling it into the boat. Apparently the motor was tied to the dory with a rope just in case it got knocked off, and Dom had simply reeled it in.

Between the two of them, they wrestled it over the side. But as soon as it was safely aboard, Alicia again collapsed with a combination of exhaustion and relief. She didn't think she'd be able to move again for some time, but she was wrong.

"Grab a paddle," Dom commanded, apparently unmoved by her paralytic condition. "We're not out of the woods yet."

"Can't we use the motor?" she objected even as she marshaled her strength and located one of the oars, fastened to the sides of the boat.

He laughed humorlessly. "Not once it's taken a salt-water dunking. Now row. Head for that closest island. We may still beat the rain."

She followed his orders, rudely issued though they were, allowing her irritation with him to fuel her depleted energy reserves. Yes, he should have been born in another century. He would have made a great Captain Bligh.

After a few minutes of mindless rowing, Alicia thought her arms were going to fall off, and the cursed little island never seemed to get any closer. But the storm clouds had. The sky had become frighteningly black, and the wind whipped her hair.

She put more oomph into her efforts. By now the burning in her muscles had given way to numbness, anyway.

"Okay, you can stop," Dom said.

She sighed thankfully, taking his words at face value. She didn't question the fact that they were still a long way from the beach, she just pulled her oar out of the water, dropped it in the bottom of the boat and tried to rub some feeling back into her arms.

Dom went over the side, alighting in water only thigh-deep, and waded to shore with the dugout in tow. When the boat touched bottom, Alicia tumbled out of it and helped to drag it up on the beach. That done, she promptly sank onto the sand in a nerveless heap. She had been strong for as long as she could. Now all she wanted was for someone to take care of everything, including her.

When the first fat raindrop pelted her face, she was sure the forces of nature were conspiring to kill her. They certainly weren't going to let her rest. This storm didn't appear to be any garden variety monsoon; the wind roared past her ears, and each droplet of rain that hit stung her skin. She and Dom would have to find shelter, and fast.

She pulled herself together and stood once again. She found Dom rummaging through what was left of the contents of the boat.

"We lost the radio, the drinking water, the ice—and my fishing pole, dammit," he said. "But we still have beer and chocolate."

Alicia briefly examined their meager provisions, zeroing in on a rusty machete, a blue plastic tarpaulin and some rope. "We'll need some type of shelter, don't you think?" she ventured.

"Yeah, right." He eyed the clouds dubiously. "Grab on to the nearest palm tree, sweetie, 'cause that's all we have on this little spit of sand."

"That's what you think," she said, finding stamina she never knew she had. She planned to issue a few orders of her own to Captain Bligh. She reached for the machete and handed it to him. "Go cut me some palm fronds—as many as you can carry. Leave the rest to me. And don't call me sweetie." She collected the tarp and rope.

"You're going to build us a shelter?" he asked. "You, who've never been camping until three days ago?"

"That's right," she said. "I *am* an engineer."

"An engineer who builds staplers and desk lamps."

"Just cut the fronds." She stalked off to find a couple of likely-looking trees to support the lean-to she planned to build. The scale might be a little different than she was used to, but the principles were the same.

Dom did as she'd asked. At least she was walking and talking and thinking. She'd scared him a few minutes ago, when she'd looked and acted more like a drowned puppy than the strong, capable Alicia he'd come to know. He'd had to fight some very powerful instincts to stop himself from dropping everything and going to her aid. Only the severity of the situation had prevented him from doing so.

They could easily have died a few minutes ago. And it was his fault. He never should have navigated so close inland when the water was rough. His desire to spare Alicia from seasickness had skewed his judgment.

The incident only served to remind Dom that it was foolish for him to entertain notions about her. A child with a delicate constitution—that's what he'd labeled her the moment he'd laid eyes on her. And though she was definitely a woman, and had proved herself much stronger than he'd originally thought, that didn't mean she could ever belong here.

After he had cut a huge armload of palm fronds, he found her in a tight grove of trees, stringing rope in and around them with her strong, capable hands. He paused for a moment to savor the sight of her, alive and vibrant. He'd almost lost her, and that realization brought a tightness to his chest. When had he come to cherish her so dearly?

Though she worked in an area sheltered somewhat from the elements, the worsening rain had plastered her T-shirt to her skin. Did she realize that the shirt delineated every curve of her small, perfect breasts, or that the cool wind had caused her nipples to harden into taut peaks?

"Don't just stand there like a ninny, help me," she said.

That was the Alicia he knew, he thought, hiding his grin as he jumped to her aid. Together they laced the fronds through the network of rope, forming a roof that sloped to the ground and walls on two sides. As they worked, Dom continued to suppress the totally inappropriate smile that threatened to show itself. She was all womanly softness, and tough as tree bark when she wanted to be.

When they completed the roof and walls, Alicia covered the whole business with the tarp, which she anchored securely with long strips of grass she'd found growing on the beach.

"It looks like something from *Gilligan's Island*," he observed skeptically.

"If you don't like it, you can stand out in the rain," she retorted as she crawled inside, giving him a terrific view of her tush.

He fully intended to join her, but not without provisions. A trip back to the boat to retrieve the beer and candy bars allowed him to get control of his physical response to her. He returned to the shelter just as the skies opened up, dropping a drenching rain.

The little lean-to was cozy, he had to admit as he tied down one corner of the tarp to form a tent flap of sorts. Earlier he had doubted the real need for shelter, figuring they were already wet, so what did it matter if they got wetter? But the storm outside sounded miserable, and he was glad he was out of it, perched on a log next to Alicia.

"The floor's going to get wet," he observed.

"Yes, well, can't have everything," she said, sitting primly with her hands folded in her lap. "I think it's a pretty good shelter, for a first effort."

Dom laughed at that, a genuine laugh. "Yes, it is," he agreed. "Would you like a beer?"

She relaxed visibly. "I'd love one. My mouth is full of salt and sand."

She unstrapped her sodden day pack from her waist and set it out of the way as he opened a bottle for each of them. The liquid was barely cool, but at least it washed away the salt taste from his mouth. He drank half of one of the small bottles in one draught. Alicia, he noticed, took several long swallows before taking the bottle from her lips.

They drank in silence for a while as nature unleashed its anger all around them. Rain slashed at their shelter as the tarp flapped and snapped in the wind. Water ran under their feet. But the shelter held up, protecting its occupants from the worst of the elements.

She drained the last of her beer and set the bottle aside. "Sounds like the storm's letting up," she said.

Dom duck-walked to the shelter's opening and stuck his head out. "You're right. The sky is clearing to the east."

"Then we can head back to Coconut Cay soon?" she asked, her expression so serious and earnest that it unnerved him.

"Um," he said, trying to think of a way to break the news to her. But he didn't have to.

"We're stuck here, aren't we?" she said.

He nodded grimly. "For tonight, at least. Even if the weather calms down, we don't have enough daylight to get back to Coconut Cay without a motor. It's a long way to row. We can try it in the morning, though."

"Try it?"

He wanted to reassure her, but he couldn't be anything less than honest. "I'm not sure about the currents. Rowing might be impossible."

"Then we really are marooned?" she asked, her voice taking on an edge of hysteria. "We don't have any food, any water."

"We have coconuts and coconut milk. And don't forget beer and chocolate. Anyway, we won't be marooned for long. If we don't show up tomorrow morning, Ginny will send Renaldo to check on us. When he sees that we left the village, he'll follow the island chain and eventually find us."

"What if Renaldo's not around?" Alicia asked worriedly. "His comings and going are rather unpredictable."

"If not him, someone will find us. Boats come by here all the time. We'll flag one down."

She didn't look reassured, not in the slightest.

"We'll be fine, I promise you," he tried again. "Just think of this as an adventure. Someday you'll have an exciting story to tell your children." A picture flashed in his mind, an image of Alicia, her body rounded in pregnancy. He would never see that. The realization caused a stab of emotion to pierce right through his soul. He'd never before felt cheated over the fact that he probably wouldn't have children. He did now.

Alicia reached for another beer, then opened it with slow, methodical movements. "I'm scared, Dom." Her voice shook.

He took her hand and absently stroked the back of it as he searched for something to say that might ease her mind. "There's no reason to be scared. We'll...we'll build a campfire, and toast coconuts for dinner. Then we can tell stories by the fire, get a good night's rest—"

"Sleeping where?" she interrupted, her every muscle tensed.

"On palm fronds, of course. The wind will dry them out, and we can cut them after dinner. Then, in the morning, we can get an early start. The water should be nice and calm, and we'll launch the boat and head for—"

"No!" She jerked her hand away from his light grasp.

"I beg your pardon?"

"*You* can tell stories and cut palm fronds. And *you* can damn well launch the frigging boat and row to China if you want. *I'm* not moving." She burst into tears, and her whole body shook with the force of her seismic sobs.

Dom was at a total loss. What had he said wrong?

"I'm sick to death of this survivalist crap," she went on. "My hands have blisters on top of blisters and every muscle in my body aches. Do you know how much I hate fish? Well I hate coconut twice as much. I won't eat it. Do you hear me? I'll starve first!"

"Alicia—"

"I hate sleeping in a tent in a damp sleeping bag. I hate mud and tarantulas and centipedes—and crabs! Those little ones that hang off the trees are disgusting, and then there's one the size of a Volkswagen that keeps me awake every night. And that awful dory of yours—just thinking about it makes me seasick. I'll live on this stupid island the rest of my life before I'll climb into that boat again."

She was very nearly hysterical. Dom briefly considered slapping her, but couldn't bring himself to do it. So he watched and waited and listened, knowing she would eventually wind herself down. Meanwhile, every complaint she lodged about life in Belize cut him to the quick. This was no place for her—he knew it with utter certainty this time.

Eventually her tirade degenerated into sobs and tears, and he could think of nothing to do except hold her. She resisted his embrace at first, which didn't surprise him. Her list of grievances included him—the way he ordered her about, expecting her to work like a pack mule and never offering any words of thanks or praise. Apparently in her eyes he embodied the essence of everything bad in Belize. But he persisted, eventually cajoling her into his arms.

She cried on his shoulder until she was spent.

"I'm sorry, Dom," she finally said, her voice muffled against his chest. "I'm just scared, that's all. I've been scared since this morning, starting when I thought Del was really in danger. And then that storm, and the boat capsized and I thought that you'd drowned and I was soon to follow—"

"Shh," he soothed, stroking her hair. She shivered, and he held her more tightly, trying to warm her with his own body heat. Again he was struck by how small and fragile she was. Her damp, rain-washed hair felt soft against his cheek.

"I've had to be strong over the past few days," she said. "And today I had to keep going because I knew if I didn't we might drown. But I don't have any strength left inside me. I can't do anything else."

"You don't have to. I'll take care of you," he said, and he meant it. He'd been much too tough on her. In trying to convince her to leave the island he'd acted like a brute. And when she'd exceeded all of his expectations, he still hadn't let up. He'd just made it harder and harder on her, as if to see how much it would take to bring her down.

Maybe he'd been testing her, hoping she might prove herself tough enough to survive this harsh place. Well, now he knew. She was an exceptional woman, but not without her limits. He'd driven her past those limits; if she hated this place it was his own doing.

Things would be different from now on, he vowed. For whatever brief time they had left together, he would treat her like the refined lady she was. "What can I do to make you feel better?" he asked, tenderly stroking her back. "Can I get you something? Another beer, maybe? Chocolate?"

"How about a hot shower, an ice-cold glass of Chablis, and a soft bed with clean sheets?" she mumbled, raising her face so that her breath was warm against his neck.

"Mmm," was all he said, since it was obvious he couldn't provide those luxuries for her. In truth, the things she'd described didn't sound half bad to him, either. Over the years, he'd spent more and more of his time in fieldwork, visiting his barren apartment in Tucson only long enough to write up the results of his research or deal with the red tape necessary to finance expeditions. But much as he loved his work here, he did miss some things about civilization.

And much as he hated to release Alicia, he knew he had to. She was too desirable, her soft mouth too close to his. "The rain's stopped," he said, easing himself away from her. "I'm going to build a fire."

"I'll help," she said immediately, but a firm pair of hands on her shoulders prevented her from rising from the log.

"You will not," he said firmly. "You will sit here and rest. Or you can come outside, if you like, but you aren't doing any work."

"Dom," she objected, "don't be silly. I didn't mean—"

"You aren't lifting a finger," he said adamantly.

"All right," she said, only because she was too drained to argue with him. "I'll come out and watch, then."

He actually helped her out of the shelter, then insisted she sit on the trunk of a fallen tree while he built a fire. Was this the same man who had so tersely ordered her to row his boat? The same man who had expected her to carry a ton of stuff on her back and trudge through a swamp? Her recent temper tantrum must have really unnerved him, to prompt such tender consideration from him. Maybe he was afraid she was going over the edge.

The tantrum had been a long time in coming, she thought as she looked out over the cool blue ocean. She'd been holding in her feelings for days, pretending that nothing bothered her. But just like a storm cloud that grows darker and heavier with rain, she eventually had to burst. She'd had her back up against a wall of pure frustration. Something had to give.

She was sorry Dom had to be the recipient of her diatribe. He hadn't done anything to deserve such abuse; he just happened to be in the way. Then again, maybe it was a sign of trust that she'd let him see her at her worst, at her most vulnerable. That was a privilege she usually reserved for her grandfather.

The last time she'd done something like this was a couple of months ago, when she'd let loose with a scorching tirade in Eddie J.'s office. She'd lambasted everything from her secretary to the food in the lunchroom vending machines . . . and then had resigned—several times over.

Her grandfather could only chuckle at her, which just infuriated her further—until she saw how ridiculous she was and began to laugh at herself. He knew her well enough to realize that such a tantrum was merely the way she dealt with built-up stress. She didn't really *mean* any of the terrible things she blurted out in the heat of anger. She was only venting frustrations. And just as today's violent storm had passed, leaving behind a calming sea and a fresh, rainwashed breeze, her own storm of anger left in its wake an inner peace and new reserves of strength.

She watched as Dom gathered wood for the fire. Most of it was damp, but he cut open some old coconuts and used the combustible fibers inside as kindling. That, and a bit of gasoline from the boat engine, and he soon had a bright blaze.

For a while Alicia enjoyed just sitting and doing nothing as the sun set behind her, turning the sky into brilliant shades of gold and fiery orange. The glorious sight reminded her that, while this place afforded many hardships, it also offered her moments of incomparable beauty. She pulled off her socks and her one remaining shoe, wiggled her toes in the sand, and inhaled of the salty breeze.

Dom was another glorious sight she wouldn't see anyplace but Belize. She savored the view she had of him, pacing around the fire, bending and straightening, his muscles bunching, then relaxing beneath the softly worn denim of his jeans. His shirt wasn't quite so white as before, and apparently he'd lost a few buttons during today's ordeal. She eyed with interest the tempting slice of sun-bronzed chest revealed by his open shirtfront.

After a few minutes of just sitting and watching Dom tend the fire, however, she grew restless. Not that she couldn't have watched him for many more hours—she would never get tired of that. But she wanted—no, *needed*—to make herself useful. She wasn't the type to sit and let other people do for her, despite what she'd told him earlier, and she had to make him understand that.

She stood decisively and walked to where the machete was stuck blade-first into the sand.

He heard her and turned, apparently surprised to see her moving about. "What do you think you're doing?" he demanded. "You're supposed to be resting."

"I'm going to make us a bed," she said with a shy smile.

Dom could only stare at her, his mouth hanging open.

"If we're going to spend the night here, I intend to do it…comfortably." She drew out the last word. Let him chew on that awhile, she mused as she pranced off in search of palm fronds. She couldn't imagine why she'd panicked earlier at the thought of being marooned on a deserted island with Dominic Seeger. Now, she couldn't envision anything more ideal.

Palm fronds were one commodity never in short supply on these islands, Alicia thought as she whacked off dozens of them and carried them back to the shelter. The sand floor inside the lean-to was damp from rain run-off, but firm. She arranged the fronds in a crisscrossing pattern until they were several layers thick. Then she lay down on them, testing out the newly made bed.

Not nearly soft enough, she decided, and some of the thick stems poked her in the back. Using her pocket knife, she shaved off the softer parts of the leaves and discarded the stems, then went back outside to cut a few more.

When she'd doubled the pallet's thickness and safely buried all the hard stems, she tried out the bed again, this time imagining Dom lying beside her. She didn't even bother to censor the fantasy, for she'd arranged their bed with all the care of a woman planning a grand seduction, and she'd known it all along.

She laughed aloud, grabbing two handfuls of the soft green leaves and letting them shower down on her. As bad as she'd felt earlier, that was as good as she felt right now. She couldn't explain it, but there it was.

"Alicia?"

She jumped and looked up to see Dom, leaning down on one knee and peering quizzically at her through the shelter opening. One final giggle escaped before she straightened up, and she could feel her face growing warm.

"Are you okay?" he asked.

"Never better," she replied breezily. "Want another beer?"

"Uh, yeah, sure."

She opened one and handed it to him, then opened another for herself, even though the first two had gone straight to her head.

"That's a nice bed you've created," he said. "I'm sure you'll be very comfortable."

"And you won't be?" she queried, raising one eyebrow.

"Oh, I expect I'll find some place soft to catch a few winks," he said carefully. "Um, just how many of those beers have you had?"

"I made this bed for both of us," she said, ignoring his question. "It would be ridiculous for you to sleep outside. There's no place comfortable and it might rain again. We both need a good night's sleep if we're going to row that boat all the way to Coconut Cay tomorrow."

"A very sound argument," he said. "But no dice. Alicia, I wouldn't sleep a wink lying next to you. Surely you can figure out why." He withdrew and returned to his fire, scowling.

She followed him. "I want to sleep with you," she said succinctly. "I want to be safe and warm in your arms." She watched his face to see what effect her words had on him.

He closed his eyes for a moment, and the muscles around his mouth tightened almost imperceptibly. "Honey, you wouldn't be anywhere near safe in my arms," he said harshly.

"I don't want to be *that* safe."

He stared intently at her, as if he was sure he'd misunderstood her.

She stared back boldly. "I want you," she said, so that there would be no mistaking her intent.

"I want you, too," he responded without hesitation. "And you, if anyone, should know how impossible this is."

"All I know is we have tonight, and I don't want to waste it."

"And all I know is I can't handle just one night with you. I would want more—" He stopped himself.

"What is it you're afraid of?" she asked softly. She was determined that this time he would tell her.

He hesitated, poking at the fire with a stick. "I'm afraid of falling in love with you, dammit. I think I'm already halfway there."

His admission sent an unexpected thrill coursing through her, and yet the ominous tone of his voice scared her silly. "Would that be so terrible?" she asked quietly.

"Yes. It would be the worst thing that could happen to me, to us. I should think that would be obvious to you."

"It isn't obvious at all."

"Alicia, we have the next few days together—that's it. If you'd stop and think about it—"

"I don't want to think about it," she said, knowing even as the words left her lips that she was being foolishly careless. But something had changed inside her today, something that made her forget caution and consequences. Perhaps it was the knowledge of her own mortality that made her want to live for the moment. "I want to make love. Why do we have to look any further ahead than that?"

"I have to look ahead. Because if we get any more tangled up, I'll have to make a choice, and I'm not sure I can live with that."

"What . . . what do you mean?" she asked with a sinking in the pit of her stomach. He was turning her down.

"You've done something to me. You've made me want things, things that I never . . . Alicia, I could give up everything for a woman like you. I could let you pull me away from my fieldwork, exactly as my father allowed Amy to do. He learned to accept what he gave up. I'm not sure I could. I think it might destroy me."

Eight

Alicia didn't understand his reasons for refusing her, but she had to respect them. This was not some manufactured excuse; his fear was very real, evident in every taut line of his body.

"All right," she said softly, wishing now that she'd never spoken up. She wanted to erase the tension she'd caused, but didn't have the slightest idea how to even try. "It was just a thought."

Whatever had happened between his father and step-mother, it must have had a devastating effect on Dominic, Alicia reasoned. Perhaps she could get him to talk about it, but she'd save that for later. Now all she wanted was to put his mind at ease and restore harmony between them.

"I'm hungry," she said after an awkward silence. "Didn't you say something about toasting coconuts?"

He stopped poking at the fire long enough to stare at her

as if she'd suggested eating live coals. "I thought you hated coconut."

She shrugged. "I've never had one right out of the shell before. I understand it tastes different from the dry, shredded kind."

He nodded slowly. "I'll see what I can do."

She watched with interest as he whacked several coconuts in half with the machete. Then they both used their pocket knives to shave off thin layers of the moist, white meat, which Dom skewered with sharp sticks. He built two coconut "shish-kebabs" and handed one to Alicia. They toasted their strange dinner over the fire.

When Dom declared them done, Alicia took a tentative bite. "Interesting," she said, which was about all she could give it. It was kind of chewy. But sandwiched between two pieces of chocolate, and washed down with another beer, it wasn't half bad.

"I never knew you were such a talented cook," she said when she'd licked the last bit of chocolate off her fingers.

"I don't know about talented. Innovative, maybe."

She could tell his heart wasn't in the conversation. In fact as he stared into the fire it appeared his thoughts were far away from here. She so wanted to go to him, to put her arms around those strong shoulders and hold him close, to chase away whatever demons haunted him just as he'd done for her. But he'd made his wishes quite clear—he didn't want her that close.

"I know it's early," she said, "but I think I'll turn in. Almost drowning has a way of wearing a body out."

"Yeah," he agreed solemnly.

"Listen, if you change your mind and decide you'd like some shelter, you're welcome to join me," she said quickly, letting the words tumble out before she lost her courage. "I promise I'll keep my hands to myself. Your virtue's safe."

She stood and brushed the sand from the back of her shorts,

hoping she could keep her word. Then she turned and started toward the lean-to, thinking how big and lonely her bed of fronds would seem now.

"Good night, then," he said. "Oh, Alicia..."

She paused and turned.

"You've been great through all this, and I'm sorry I let it happen. If I'd been more careful—"

"Don't blame yourself, please," she said. "You couldn't have known the weather would take such a nasty turn—just like I couldn't have known Del would get sick. You wouldn't let me blame myself for that, remember?"

He nodded and stared down at the toes of his battered shoes.

"No one can anticipate every fluke fate throws at us. And anyway, I'm not sorry it happened." She turned and continued on her way.

Dom watched her go, watched the way her hips swayed provocatively as she walked barefoot through the sand, and puzzled over her attitude. Earlier, he'd have sworn she hated him, this island and the whole damn country with a murderous passion. Now she seemed perfectly accepting.

She was a confusing woman. And she no doubt considered him a confusing man. His own behavior didn't make a lot of sense, not even to him. What man would turn down a night of passion with *her?*

But though he'd been deeply moved by her invitation, and the obvious desire that had sparked in the depths of her night-sky eyes, every self-preservational instinct within him had clamored to be heard: Don't make love to her. Don't, or you'll never be able to let her go.

A couple of days ago he would have given in to temptation. But the stakes were higher, now that he knew how profoundly she affected him. The things he feared were so close he could almost touch them.

He stayed up hours after Alicia left, staring alternately into the fire and out to sea, letting his thoughts chase one another in a game of tag that nobody won. Sometimes his gaze strayed to the little shelter he and Alicia had built. If he tried very hard to block out certain thoughts, he could almost convince himself to go to her, to accept and enjoy what she'd offered him. But only almost.

Judging from the position of the moon, high overhead, he guessed it was almost midnight when he finally decided to sleep. He stretched out in the sand near the fire with the machete within easy reach, crooked his arm to cradle his head and closed his eyes. He'd slept in worse places.

He awoke some time later, disoriented, unsure what had disturbed him. Then he heard a faint, mewling cry, and all of his senses were on instant alert. The noise came from the shelter.

All vestiges of sleep vanished as he lurched to his feet and grabbed the machete. Ten long paces and he was there, his mind filled with every horrible thing that might cause Alicia distress—tarantulas, scorpions, snakes—did this island have snakes? Some did and some didn't.

He ripped the flap open and dived inside. "Alicia?"

She didn't answer. All was quiet.

"Alicia?" he said again as he pulled out the disposable lighter he always kept in his jeans pocket, and flicked it to life. It became instantly apparent that Alicia was not in any grave danger. In fact, she was asleep.

Dom extinguished the lighter and fell back on the leafy pallet, breathing in great gulps of air. His heart still beat double time, but the rhythm gradually slowed as relief overtook him. She'd cried out in her sleep, that was all. She'd been dreaming.

He wondered then what night terrors plagued her. The moon, now low in the sky, shined brightly through the open flap, faintly illuminating her face. He propped himself up on one elbow and studied her. Her delicate features, reposed in sleep, looked at peace now, and her breathing was slow and rhythmic.

He couldn't help but study the rest of her, then regretted it. Her T-shirt had ridden up high on her ribs, exposing her slender torso to the moon's silvery glow. The soft underside of one breast was barely visible, peaking out milky white beneath the shirt's hem.

He wanted to touch her stomach. He knew it would be soft as talcum powder, and warm. He moved his hand, holding it aloft several inches above her sleeping form, and actually would have touched her if she hadn't moaned softly.

He jerked his hand back and studied her face with renewed concern, but she didn't seem to be distressed. She sighed, shivered slightly, then abruptly flopped over onto her stomach. She stretched one arm out, then let it drop, her hand landing distressingly near a very sensitive part of Dom's anatomy.

He bit his lip to stifle the groan that threatened to escape. Good Lord, how had he gotten himself into this? And how would he explain it if she woke up?

He watched and waited, hoping she would remove her hand. She grew more restless, making soft, drowsy sounds and wiggling her bottom as if trying to get comfortable, but her hand remained possessively splayed across his pelvis, and his jeans grew more uncomfortable with every passing second.

When he could stand it no longer, he gingerly grasped her wrist and tucked her hand up by her shoulder, where it ought to be. He breathed a sigh of relief when she didn't stir and prepared to withdraw from the shelter. But he couldn't resist touching her, just once.

He let his hand rest lightly between her shoulder blades, then ran his fingertips down the center of her back to the bare skin at her waist. It was every bit as soft and warm as he'd anticipated. He pulled his hand away and bent to place a kiss, light as a hummingbird's wing, at the small of her back. Then he closed his eyes and, with every ounce of willpower he possessed, pulled away.

That's when he saw the gleam of one open, drowsy blue eye, staring at him.

She turned her head then and he saw both eyes, reflecting surprise and wonder, joy and anticipation. "You changed your mind?" she whispered.

There was no way he could tell her no, not while she looked at him with that sweet, vulnerable expression. He was lost, drowning, and unable to make even the slightest effort to save himself.

Without speaking, he reached out to smooth her glossy hair away from her face. He wanted to say something, anything, but the words didn't come.

Apparently words weren't necessary, not for Alicia. She reached up and grasped his hand firmly, then brought his palm to her lips. It was such a sweet gesture, yet just that faint touch of her mouth set his blood on fire.

He longed to take her in his arms and kiss her senseless, to drown in the feel of her bareness against his, her womanly scent, her breath warm against his face. But at the same time he was almost paralyzed with indecision—not whether to stay or go, for that choice had been made, for better or worse. But now that their lovemaking was inevitable, he had no idea how to proceed.

He'd never thought this far ahead before. She was such a fragile creature, and he was a big man unaccustomed to gentleness. He'd shared nights of sex with women before, but he'd never truly *made* love to a woman he cared about. What if he hurt her?

As if sensing his hesitancy, she rolled over to one side and ran her hand up his arm to his shoulder, then began a slow massage. Taking a cue from her, he did the same, rubbing her neck, her firm upper arms, her back. They explored each other leisurely, their caresses eventually becoming more intimate.

It was a strange and very pleasurable way to initiate love-making, Dom thought through a haze of desire. He'd always imagined that if they came together, it would be with an explosive burst of passion. Perhaps that's what would have happened if he hadn't just awakened her from a sound sleep.

She inhaled sharply when his hand slid under her T-shirt to cup her breast. He touched the hardened peak, tentatively at first, then rolled it between his thumb and forefinger. She shivered and made a sound that he took for approval. Excited and encouraged by her response, he leaned over and took her nipple into his mouth, kissing gently.

She trembled, and he experienced a purely male sense of satisfaction that he had the power to excite her. At the same time, he knew her power over him was twice as strong. That point was brought intensely home as she came more fully awake, and her strong, clever fingers touched his arousal, still uncomfortably trapped inside his jeans.

The last thing he wanted to do was move too fast; in fact, he intended to make their intimacy last as long as humanly possible. But if she touched him like that again he was going to explode. Attempting to distract her, he guided her hand away as he moved his mouth to her other breast. She expelled a deep breath as he circled the taut aureole with his tongue, and her hand strayed back, intent on playing with fire.

He groaned and pulled away from her, lying back. "Time out," he said. "Excuse me while I think about a brick wall for a few seconds, okay? Because if I don't..."

She sat up, and he could see that she was smiling. "You don't have to slow down on my account," she said as she pulled her T-shirt over her head, then reached for the fastening on her shorts. "Now that I'm awake, I'm in no mood to take my time."

And he had no intention of rushing, he wanted to say. But as he watched her shimmy out of her shorts, all thoughts of brick walls fled and he knew she could have him any way she saw fit.

She unfastened the only two remaining buttons on his shirt, and he sat up so she could ease it off his shoulders. He winced when she inadvertently rubbed a scrape on his ribs.

Alicia immediately sensed his pain. "You're hurt," she said.

"Got scraped on the coral," he said matter-of-factly. "It's nothing."

She discarded his shirt, then leaned over him. She didn't kiss the injury itself, for the skin was raw, but she kissed all around it. Her soft lips forged a hot trail up and down his ribs, straying across his nipples and down his belly. The sting of his injury was quickly forgotten.

The jeans had to go, and with one swift movement he ripped open the button fly and slid the denim down his hips and legs. The cool night breeze caressed the heated length of him, followed shortly thereafter by the surprise of Alicia's warm mouth.

"Good Lord, Alicia, what are you doing to me?" He was supposed to be making love to her, and instead she had him flat on his back and paralyzed with the need for her touch.

Her maddening caress slowed. She abandoned him for a moment, but then she was lying beside him, her head on his shoulder. "I'm sorry," she whispered. "I don't mean to be so... I don't know what came over me. Suddenly I just wanted to taste you all over..."

"Oh, honey, don't apologize," he said hoarsely. "That was...that felt...honestly, I wasn't objecting." He realized then that they were lying against each other, naked, and he hadn't once kissed her mouth. He remedied that situation, cupping her delicate jaw in his hand and taking gentle possession of her soft, soft mouth with his. Their tongues touched lightly, then swirled together in a passionate dance. No kiss had ever reached so deeply into his soul.

"Do you want me to keep doing what I was doing before?" she asked guilelessly.

Was it possible she didn't know how close she'd brought him to the edge? "Alicia, if you do that again I'm going to lose it before I...before we..."

"Then let's make love," she said, but her voice shook.

It occurred to him that she might not be ready yet, despite her stated impatience and bold behavior. He slid his hand down her back, over her deliciously rounded hip, and to the nest of soft curls between her thighs. Her legs were tightly closed to him, and he guessed then that she was a little afraid.

He stroked her thighs with his fingertips, and after a few moments he could feel her relax and opening to him. He cupped her mound in his palm, then tentatively touched her most secret place. She smiled and moaned simultaneously when he slid one finger inside her. She was most definitely ready.

"I don't want to wait any longer," she pleaded.

That was all he needed to hear.

She held her arms open to him as he covered her body with his, then clung to him with a charming show of need. Poised at the brink of her womanhood, he hesitated. She was so small. Besides being afraid he might crush her with his weight, he again experienced a terrible fear that in his urgency he would hurt her.

So he tried to go slowly. But she wouldn't let him. The moment he started to enter her, she grasped him firmly, one hand on each buttock, and pulled him to her.

He buried himself in her warmth. She cried out, but it was no cry of pain.

He began to move and she followed his lead, tilting her hips up to eagerly meet each thrust. Several times he had to slow her down. He'd never felt anything as exquisite as having Alicia all around him, and he didn't want it to end.

She was so precious, and for this moment, at least, she was his. He kissed her, a kiss that marked her as his, a kiss of utter possession.

She nibbled at his lower lip, and for some reason that one playful gesture shattered his control. A wave of indescribable pleasure rolled through him, and then he was over the summit, falling fast. The sensation of falling was so real he gasped for air and his head reeled. But he landed gently when it was over, pressed against Alicia's warm body. She shuddered slightly beneath him, her breathing as labored as his.

He suspected that she had shared his ecstasy, but he was ashamed to admit that he wasn't sure. He'd been so attuned to the intense sensations flooding his own body that he hadn't devoted much conscious thought to her pleasure.

That realization shamed him even more. Such an exquisite woman deserved a skillful lover, one who could do justice to her spectacular body—and he was no Don Juan. But she could inspire him to learn. He would take great satisfaction in learning every nuance of her body.

He would never get that chance. Tonight was all they had. A pain as sharp as a knife point sliced through his chest.

"Oh, Dom," she said on a sigh, still holding him tightly.

"Oh, what?" he asked with his face buried against her neck.

She wasn't sure what she wanted to say. There simply were no appropriate words. She shivered with the last vestiges of her climax. She'd never felt anything like what his love-making did to her—wave after wave of mindless pleasure, and then, when she'd felt him nearing the peak, a final explosion of warmth and fiery little tingles over every square inch of her skin. She didn't want to let him go, ever.

"Aren't I crushing you?" he asked with touching concern.

"No. Stay." She wasn't yet capable of wordy responses.

"All right. I'm not going anywhere."

Sated and warm, and reassured by his words, she fell asleep in Dom's arms.

Alicia awoke as the sun's first rays struck the shelter, casting a blue-green light through the tarp and palm fronds that formed the walls and ceiling. She yawned and stretched, wondering at first why she was sore from her head to her feet. The memories of yesterday bombarded her—the boat, the waves, the panic of near death. She'd dreamed of it last night.

A rustling next to her alerted her to Dom's presence. She turned her head, wondering idly why he was naked—and why she was in the same condition. Then more memories came to the surface, beautiful, pleasurable ones this time. She stifled a gasp as she remembered her wanton behavior, then smiled involuntarily, recalling Dom's passion, which he tempered so well with tenderness and concern for her comfort.

She sat up so she could really look at him. He lay on his back, one knee bent, one arm flung over his eyes to block the increasing light. He was a beautiful male, strong and tanned, his muscles carved to a sharp definition from hard work.

With exacting clarity she remembered what his body felt like: firm and uncompromising. She wanted to touch him again, but she wouldn't risk waking him, not yet. With morning came other concerns—getting off this island, for instance. With morning came the end of the spell that had held them last night. But for these few minutes, at least, he was hers.

Her mind, still drowsy and unguarded, began to wander. She'd always believed she was the maker of her own destiny. Did she really have to leave Belize so soon? She had several weeks of vacation built up. She could stay on. Surely, as far behind as the excavation was, Dom wouldn't turn down her offer to stay awhile and work.

But eventually "awhile" would come to an end. She would have to return to her home and her career in Houston, where she was needed, where she belonged. She could never abandon the company, or her grandfather. Eddie J. had given her too much, taught her everything. One of the things he'd taught her was loyalty.

Dom could no more change his life than she could hers. His place was here. To pry him away from his fieldwork and try to mold him into an urban dweller would be cruel.

A sadness welled up from somewhere deep inside, spreading over her, engulfing her. Tears pooled in her eyes, and she let them run down her cheeks unchecked. Dominic Seeger was the best man she'd ever found—strong, intelligent, compassionate, with a will of his own, and enough guts to live the life other men only dreamed of. And she couldn't have him.

Now she understood something of the fears he harbored. Now she had a glimpse of the pain she would suffer, when forced to return to the life she'd already made for herself and abandon the one she wished desperately she could have.

The tears passed after a few minutes. She dried her eyes with the back of her hand, relieved that Dom hadn't seen her crying. She wouldn't want him to think she regretted what had passed between them.

Staring at his sleeping form had its merits, but she decided she preferred him conscious. She picked up a leafy frond and tickled his chest hairs with it. He brushed it away. She tickled him lower, then lower still, giggling quietly at her own audacity.

His eyes flew open and he grabbed her hand. "What is it you think you're doing?" he demanded. But a lazy smile soon gave him away. He wasn't at all displeased to have her wake him in such a playful manner.

When she answered his question with a self-conscious grin, he pulled her off balance until she had no choice but to fall against him. "Good morning," he said just before giving her a leisurely kiss.

"Mmm, definitely a good morning," she said when she regained her voice. "I'm glad you're in a pleasant mood. I can't stand people who wake up grumpy."

"Me? Grumpy? Never. Well, not today, anyway." He kissed the tip of her nose. "Damn, you wake up beautiful."

She felt the blood rush to her face, and she was suddenly much too aware of her disastrously unkempt hair and the breasts she'd always thought too small and the legs that earned her the nickname "Chicken Legs" in grade school. She'd never thought of herself as beautiful. But the way Dom was looking at her, she could almost believe it. She felt extremely desirable, at any rate.

"I was afraid you'd regret what happened last night," she said on a more serious note. "Earlier you were so positive that it was the wrong thing—"

He silenced her with another kiss. "Someday soon, I probably will regret it," he said. "But right now I don't. It was too perfect."

"It was that," she agreed, nodding for emphasis.

"I was hoping that you thought so, too," he said with a crooked smile. "Everything happened so fast. I wanted to take my time. A woman like you deserves—"

"What do you mean, 'a woman like me'?" she asked suddenly. It wasn't the first time she'd caught him using that phrase. "I'd like to think I'm unique, and you keep putting me in some sort of category."

He studied her thoughtfully. "Mmm," he said after a long silence, but then he more or less ducked the question. "I suppose you are one of a kind." His lingering gaze warmed her as he perused the length of her body. "Let's go for a swim," he suggested suddenly.

"Swim?" She'd thought perhaps they would dawdle inside their little cocoon for a while longer, reclaiming the magic they'd found last night.

"I want to see you in the sunlight," he said, his voice husky.

Well, when he put it like that... She nodded. "Okay. But I don't know about swimming. After yesterday, I'm not so sure I ever want to swim in the ocean again."

"Then just get your toes wet," he said as he sat up, wide awake now and full of energy. "Come on. We both know you're not shy."

She could feel herself blushing again, all the way down to the soles of her feet. "How rude of you to mention my unladylike behavior," she said with a laugh as she reluctantly allowed him to pull her outside into the morning sun.

They both stood, and Dom took two steps back to fully admire her. She let him, because it *was* too late for her to be shy.

"You are every inch a lady," he said softly. "I would never suggest otherwise."

They ran across the still-cool sand to the edge of the water. It was calm and blue this morning, nothing like yesterday's threatening surf, and Alicia found she was not at all reluctant to swim. They chased each other through the waves, diving in and out of the water like playful porpoises, catching each other just often enough to make the game interesting.

Alicia had never felt so in tune with nature or with her own body. Even the soreness in her muscles served to remind her how alive she was.

Dom caught her for the last time, refusing to let her go. She didn't want to be released. He kissed her hard on the mouth, like a conquering pirate, leaving no doubt as to his intentions. She returned his passion in full measure, leaving no doubt as to her unconditional surrender.

He picked her up and carried her toward the shore, his mouth never leaving hers. Just as he reached the beach, however, he stopped and set her down, distractedly breaking the kiss.

"What's wrong?" she asked.

"You don't hear it?"

"Hear what?"

"A boat motor. I think we're about to have a visitor."

"Oh." She looked down at herself. "Guess that means we have to get dressed."

He gave her a smile of sincerest regret. "Guess so. Hey, cheer up. We're about to get rescued."

"Mmm, yeah." She wasn't nearly as excited by that prospect as she should have been.

Nine

Alicia felt a wistfulness descend on her as she watched Dom pull on his jeans over wet skin. She wanted to say something that would ease the transition from the incredible intimacy they'd shared into the real world, but he grabbed his shirt and darted outside again before she could think of the right words.

She took her time dressing, letting herself air dry first before donning yesterday's rumpled shorts and shirt. She had just tied her lone shoe when she heard a familiar, brash voice.

"Alicia, are you decent?"

It was a good thing she was "decent," because a second later, Skip's blond head appeared at the shelter's entrance.

She grinned in welcome, despite her mild irritation. "Skip! I'm so glad to see you," she fibbed. She crawled outside and gave him an awkward hug. They never had been much good at showing outward affection. "How did you

find us?'' She looked toward the beach, where she saw
Renaldo talking to Dom.

"Renaldo was in the village last night. Some kid at the
marina told him that you'd taken off a while before the
storm hit, and he was afraid you'd run into trouble. He
showed up at Coconut Cay early this morning, and when
Ginny told him you'd never arrived, we went looking for
you. So what happened?''

Alicia reached inside the shelter to retrieve her pack, then
strapped it around her waist. "We lost our motor," she said
simply as she began unfastening the blue tarp. She didn't feel
like going into great detail. The panic of almost drowning
was still too fresh.

"I take it Del's okay. I heard he flew home yesterday.''

Alicia related the doctor's diagnosis, which seemed to
please Skip. "That's a relief," he said, turning his attention
to the shelter. "This is neat. Did you build it?''

"Yes, I did," she said proudly. The breeze tried to whip
the tarp out of her hands. She managed to subdue it, though
Skip, oblivious to her plight as usual, still studied the lean-
to. "Did you both sleep in there? It looks kind of...
cramped.''

She cringed. Skip was obviously intrigued by the idea of
Dom and Alicia sharing something more than a frightening
experience. Once her cousin took hold of an idea, he would
pursue it with the tenacity of a hound chasing a fox to
ground.

"We managed," she said.

"Mmm," he said, eyeing her speculatively. "What happened to your other shoe?''

"I lost it. Get that beer, would you? And the chocolate
bars,'' she instructed him curtly, nodding toward the shelter's interior. "Let's get out of here. I'm hungry and thirsty
and I'd like to change clothes.''

Skip did as she asked but continued to look thoughtful, as if he were weighing the possibilities.

Eventually he would figure it out, Alicia mused, disheartened by the thought as she stowed their remaining supplies under the bow of Dom's dory, which was now tied to the back of Renaldo's boat. Skip knew her too well, and he was very good at reading people's moods. He hadn't gone into personnel work for no good reason.

"Is that everything?" Dom asked her as he secured the old machete under the gunwales.

The question seemed to have added significance, although maybe it was her own confused emotions making her more sensitive. "I think so," she replied, swallowing the ridiculous catch in her throat.

"Let's go, then. I'll ride in my boat, to give it some weight. Otherwise it'll bounce all over the place. You can ride up front in Renaldo's."

She nodded, moving to do as he directed.

"Oh, Alicia?"

She stopped, fixing him with a gaze she was sure told him everything. She was sad to see the end of their adventure.

"Face front, and keep your eyes on the horizon. The water is smooth today, so it shouldn't be too bad."

Though she hated to be reminded about the possibility of seasickness, his concern warmed her to the core.

The trip lasted less than an hour. Alicia was actually relieved to see their familiar, mangrove-choked island with its dilapidated house. It was starting to feel like home.

Ginny greeted them at the shore. "What did you do, Dom, get lost?" she called as she helped guide Renaldo's boat up onto the beach. But Alicia could tell the older woman was relieved to see them.

"It's a long story," Dom replied dryly. "I'll tell you all about it, soon as I get a cup of coffee in my hands. Now stop harassing me and let's get the boats unloaded.'' But he offered Ginny an apologetic smile that belied his gruff words.

As Alicia lifted the remaining beer out of Dom's boat, preparing to take it to the house, she felt a sharp sting on her upper arm. She dropped the beer. "Ouch," she yelped, rubbing at her arm. "What was that?"

"What do you mean, 'what was that'?" Skip said, taking the beer she'd dropped. "It was a sand fly. They're really swarming today." He slapped at one on his neck. "You mean this is the first time you've been bitten?"

She nodded, then winced when she felt a sting on her bare leg.

"What about your moisturizer?" Ginny asked.

Alicia snapped her fingers. "I'm not wearing it," she said. "It's in my tent. I'd forgotten all about it."

By the time she made a trip to her tent, cleaned up as best she could and changed clothes, her four companions were gathered under the house, indulging in hot coffee. She tossed her oversized tube of moisturizer to Skip as she poured her own steaming cup.

"I don't know about this stuff," Skip said dubiously, opening the cap and taking a sniff. "It smells like flowers."

Ginny snatched it away from him. "I'm not proud, I'll try some," she said. "Anything to keep these cursed flies away."

In the end they all tried some, even Renaldo, but Alicia wasn't paying much attention. She'd discovered a pot warming near the fire. She removed the lid and scooped a mountain of the contents onto a plastic plate, then sat down at the table and proceeded to feast.

After several bites, she looked up to see Dom staring at her, his surprise evident. "Alicia, you're eating fish for breakfast."

She nodded. "Mmm-hmm. And beans and rice, all mixed together. Want some?"

"Uh, no thanks. I'll have bread and jam."

"Mmm, I'll have some of that, too."

"I thought you *hated* fish," he said.

"Nobody hates fish," Renaldo stated confidently.

"Acute hunger has a way of changing your perspective," she said, scraping her plate clean. She drained the last of her coffee and sighed. She felt two hundred percent better. "So, what's on the agenda today?" she asked, her gaze flicking back and forth between Dom and Ginny.

Dom cleared his throat. "Um, I thought maybe you'd like to take the day off."

"No way," Skip complained. "If I have to work, so does she. Anyway, she had yesterday off."

"She worked harder yesterday than any three grown men put together," Dom said hotly. His quick defense of her surprised Alicia. "We weren't on some picnic, you know."

"What exactly *did* happen yesterday?" Ginny asked gently. "You haven't told us."

Dom related the day's events, downplaying his own heroics and embellishing Alicia's until she sounded like Conan the Barbarian. She would have objected, but frankly she enjoyed Skip's look of awe.

"You could have died!" Skip exclaimed, and for once he seemed as if he might actually miss her.

"It wasn't that bad," she said, lying because she didn't want to revive Dom's guilt over the mishap. "Anyway, we're back safe and sound, and I have no intention of sitting around on my duff. I'm ready to dig."

"You can do lab work," Dom compromised.

"We're all caught up in the lab," Ginny objected. "Let her work with me on Dog Tooth. We'll go easy. You and Skip can play in the mud."

Dom obviously didn't like the arrangement, but couldn't think of a good enough reason to object.

It was a pleasant day, warm, dry and breezy, and Alicia hummed as she worked. She missed Dom's company—over the past few days she'd grown accustomed to his raw sexuality, tickling her senses at every turn. She missed his tender concern and even his sometimes caustic comments.

But she would see him later, and that's why she whistled. Even though the physical part of their affair was over with, she still looked forward to his stimulating presence. She probably glowed whenever she was within twenty feet of him, a condition Skip no doubt would notice. She wasn't sure she cared.

Renaldo brought them some treats for dinner—canned corned beef, bell peppers and some weird type of melon for dessert. Alicia, relieved to see something besides fish, volunteered to cook. Ginny nodded gratefully and left to bathe and enjoy some time to herself.

Using the spices Renaldo had brought her the other day, Alicia fried the beef and peppers and mixed it all up with rice to form a sort of hash. She hoped it would be good. For some reason it seemed important to prove her campfire culinary skills.

Dom, still slightly damp and fresh smelling from his recent swim, drifted close to the fire and peered into the cook pot, then inhaled deeply and smiled. "That smells wonderful," he said, and his approval pleased her inordinately.

His nearness pleased her even more. He lingered close to the fire, poking idly at it with a stick. The orange glow illuminated his strong profile, casting his face in dancing shadows.

She wanted to touch him. Did he already regret their passion? she wondered. He looked very serious. But a few moments later his eyes darted sideways toward her and he smiled mischievously.

"I've seen you in moonlight and sunlight," he said in a low voice. "I wouldn't mind seeing you in firelight, too." Then he sauntered away.

Suddenly she was too warm. He shouldn't say things like that, and she intended to tell him so. They should both be grateful for the brief but beautiful night fate had given them. Trying to steal more time together would only lead to frustration.

Everyone seemed to like the dinner, even Renaldo, who so dearly loved his fish.

"I don't know what we'd do without you, Alicia," Ginny said as she sliced the strange melon. "You're a hard worker, a great cook, you found us that nice pot, your moisturizer keeps the bugs away—and I can't believe the improvements to the outhouse. Did you see the outhouse, Dom?"

"Uh, no." He shot an amused smile at Alicia.

"It has canvas walls, now, and a door. It's downright civilized."

"There's not much to it," Alicia said. "I strung up some rope and canvas during our lunch break."

Skip glowered and remained silent. He couldn't stand it when his cousin received praise and he got nothing. Alicia suspected he was especially disappointed that he hadn't uncovered any exciting artifacts during his digging.

The melon was sweet and juicy, and Alicia savored each little bite as it melted on her tongue. But when she discovered Dom watching her with obvious interest, she quickly finished up, then took her dishes to the bucket of soapy water Ginny had made.

"I'll do those," Ginny said. "The cook is excused from dish duty."

"Thanks." All Alicia wanted was to escape to her own little tent and curl up in her own little sleeping bag. If she didn't she would be much too tempted to take what Dom so obviously offered. Just the sight of him, innocently putting their leftovers into the cooler, caused something warm and alive to quiver deep inside her.

"Going to bed so soon?" Ginny asked when she saw Alicia gathering up her pack, her flashlight and the rain poncho she kept with her constantly now, in deference to the frequent, unexpected cloudbursts.

"Unless there's something that needs doing." She suspected it wasn't yet eight o'clock, but her body had adjusted to island time. Even though she was bone tired, she'd no doubt be wide awake before dawn.

"There is one small thing you can help me with," Dom said. "The tape measure needs cleaning."

The measure he referred to was an extremely precise steel tape on a long roll, used for surveying. Exposed to the salty air, it would soon rust if someone didn't wipe it down with fresh water after each use. Cleaning it was a two-person job.

"Sure, I'll help," she said good-naturedly, even though she detected an undercurrent, a definite ulterior motive. They hadn't had a minute alone all day.

But Dom was all business as they stood in a clearing to perform the task. It was dark, but they didn't really need any light. Alicia held the end of the tape and walked out with it a good thirty meters, until he signaled for her to stop. Then she slowly walked it back as Dom reeled in the tape, wiping down each inch with wet paper towels.

When she was within a few inches of him, she let go of the tape. "There. Is that it?"

"Not quite." He set the measure against a tree, then quickly reached for her hand before she had a chance to guess his intentions. "I've thought about you all day." His voice was deliciously husky, his hand warm and rough on hers, and it muddled her thinking. He leaned against the tree and pulled her closer, so that she straddled his leg, but he didn't try to kiss her. "Talk to me, Alicia."

She cast a worried glance toward the house where Ginny still puttered around.

"They already know," Dom said softly.

"They do? Skip suspects, I think, but—"

"Skip looks at me like he'd enjoy seeing me skewered and roasted over the camp fire."

"Then you're right, he probably figured it out," she said on a dismal note. "But Ginny? Has she said anything?"

"Plenty," Dom replied without elaborating.

They stood in silence for a while, Dom's hold on her light but possessive nonetheless, causing the heat deep inside her to roil restlessly, begging to be set free. He'd been right when he said one night of passion would never be enough.

She sighed hopelessly.

"Is it so bad that they know?" he asked softly, running his finger down her cheek. His touch, so simple, made her tremble with remembered passion. "We found something wonderful between us. Could anyone begrudge us for enjoying it in this... uncomfortable place?"

"It does bother me," she answered honestly. "I told you before—I'm a very private person."

"But not shy," he teased, tracing the outline of her jaw.

"Dom, please..." But her objection wasn't very strident.

"Alicia, *please,*" he echoed, giving the word a very different meaning. "You have little more than a week left here. If I can't touch you during that week I'll go crazy."

"Eight very short days," she said glumly. Not long ago she couldn't wait until the end of her stay here. Now she dreaded it. "What do you suggest, that you sneak into my tent every night? Or that we slip away during our lunch break and rendezvous someplace in the jungle?" She shook her head. "It's impossible."

"That's not what I'm suggesting at all," he said. "I say we should be open about everything. Move your things into my tent, and to hell with what other people think." He held her by the shoulders, his grip growing stronger with each word he uttered. "You have no idea what you stirred up when you asked me to make love to you last night. I can't just turn it off. I know we have only a short time—let's make it spectacular."

"And when it's over?" She had to ask, as much for his sake as hers.

He must have realized that his hand was biting into her shoulder, because he loosened his grip and rubbed her upper arms. "Weren't you the one who didn't want to think about the future?" he asked wistfully.

"It'll get here, whether we think about it or not," she said with her customary practicality.

"It'll get here, whether we choose to follow our instincts or deny them," he countered. "At this point, saying goodbye will be just as . . . difficult, either way."

Dammit, he was making sense. "You hardly seem like the same man who was terrified of a kiss that first night," she observed.

"I wasn't terrified," he objected, hotly defending his male pride. But then he wilted a bit. "Oh, I guess maybe I was. I knew, almost from the instant I met you, that you could make me feel things I didn't want to feel. That's what I was afraid of."

"And you're not scared anymore?"

There was a long silence before he answered. "Don't kid yourself. I'm still afraid. But it's like . . . have you ever jumped out of an airplane?" he asked suddenly.

"No. Have you?"

"Once. I was scared spitless, with that paralyzing kind of fear that twists your insides up in knots. I was sure I was going to die. I almost chickened out. And then . . ." He struggled to find the words.

"And then?" she prompted.

"And then I jumped. I still thought I was going to die, that my parachute wouldn't open, or that I'd land in a tree, but somehow...I just didn't care as much. Because I was flying, and the sensation was so exhilarating, being up there with the clouds and the birds. I could have sworn I touched the sun that day. Nothing's ever come close to that feeling...until last night, Alicia. Until last night, with you."

No other words could have moved her more than those, spoken so eloquently from the heart. She moved closer to him, until her breasts were pressed against his chest, then twined her arms around his neck. Their mouths were a scant inch apart.

"I need to get a few things from my tent," she whispered.

He understood her meaning. "I'll be waiting." He kissed just the corner of her mouth before releasing her.

Back at her tent, Alicia pulled out her air mattress, her sleeping bag, a change of clothes for tomorrow and a few essentials. She brushed her teeth using water from her canteen, then gathered everything up and began negotiating her way in the dark toward Dom's tent.

"Need some help?"

She was so startled she dropped everything. "Skip! I, uh..."

"Alicia, this isn't like you," he said, sounding ominous.

She bit her lip and counted to ten. "It's not your concern," she said evenly.

"Of course it's my concern. You're family."

"And this is not a family matter," she hissed. "I intend to sleep in Dom's tent tonight...and every night until we go home," she added, having just made the decision.

"And then what?"

That was the sixty-thousand-dollar question. "Then it'll be over." But it wouldn't be, not in her heart, anyway. "And I'll be fine." But she wouldn't be, not for a long time.

"Okay, then. Just so you're not planning to drag this guy home with you and marry him, or something like that. I mean, I like Dom and everything, but I can't see him—"

"Oh, shut *up*, Skip." She simply wasn't in the mood to listen to another dismal assessment of her hopes for a future with Dom.

"All right, already." Skip actually helped her retrieve her things from the ground. "Just be careful."

Oh, go stick your head in the latrine, she wanted to retort. The only thing that stopped her was the knowledge that behind the overbearing big-brother act, her cousin really did care about her. "I'll see you in the morning," she said instead.

Dom was waiting for her in the dark tent. "I was beginning to wonder what was taking so long." He switched on his flashlight and surveyed all she'd brought with her. "Ah, now I see. Maybe we should have summoned a moving van?"

"Very funny. I'm not into minimalist camping, thank you. I got my quota of that yesterday." She arranged her air mattress and sleeping bag just so, then pulled off her boots and crawled inside, feeling ill at ease and anything but amorous.

Dom zipped the flap closed. "I don't mind. There's plenty of room for whatever you want to bring in here."

"That's good, 'cause I'm bringing the rest of it tomorrow. I'm here for the duration."

"You are?" He sounded surprised...and pleased, she hoped.

"I already told Skip."

"Ah, so that's why you're so agitated. You had a run-in with dear old cousin Skip."

"Yeah, and he acted like a complete jerk, too.... Oh, Dom, this is very hard for me. I'm just not cut out to be the brazen type."

The corner of his mouth turned up wickedly. "You could learn." He switched off the flashlight, plunging them into an intimate darkness, then placed warm hands on her shoulders.

As he started a slow massage, her passion, banked but not extinguished, suddenly sprang to life, and her encounter with Skip began to fade in significance. "I guess I'm just being silly," she said.

"You're being your normally cautious self, and believe it or not, I like that about you. You're practical as a nun, strong as a bull, and you can be tough as a coconut hull—"

"Gee, how flattering," she interjected. "That's about the most unromantic description—"

"Let me finish. You're all those things and yet so soft and delicate and feminine, like flowers and...and baby powder. Just looking at you makes my mouth go dry. Until I got to know you, I didn't believe that all of those qualities could exist in one woman." He leaned closer to her, until his warm breath fanned the back of her neck. "I doubt I'll ever encounter such a combination again."

The sincerity in his velvety voice caressed her in the darkness as surely as his hands caressed her body. She was overwhelmed by a sudden tenderness for Dom, for this man who had shunned most of the civilized world's trappings. If he felt anything for her, it wasn't her sophistication, her success, her wealth or her family connections that attracted him, as had often been the case in previous relationships. No, something intrinsic in her soul drew Dom to her. The realization gave her an emotional jolt, as well as an unbelievably strong physical rush.

She swiveled around in the small space, finding her legs suddenly tangled up in his. And he wasn't wearing a stitch, which surprised her momentarily but didn't displease her. The fire he'd ignited inside her burned white hot, and she felt an almost frantic need to join her flesh with his, to express with her lovemaking the intense emotions she couldn't put into words.

She ran a questioning hand down his bare chest, delighting in the light dusting of soft, curled hair that rubbed against her palm.

"I was getting ready for bed, and I sleep nude," he said, not at all apologetic.

"Somehow I didn't picture you in pajamas." Her voice was raspy and foreign to her own ears.

"Oh? And how do you picture me?" he asked. His breath caught as he unfastened the top button of her blouse and then the next one.

"Right now I picture you making wild love to me."

Her words ignited him. With deft fingers he finished the job of undoing her buttons, then slid the shirt down her arms and off. By the time he reached for her bra, his fingers, shaking slightly, weren't quite so deft. But just the same he managed to deal with the front clasp, freeing her small breasts from their lace confinement. They ached for his touch, and she moaned softly as he closed both hands over them. There was little that was gentle in his touch this time, just raw need, and she fed on it.

When their mouths came together, hot and hungry, the contact made her dizzy. It was a grinding, almost punishing kiss, though she couldn't complain—she was as much the instigator as he. She held his strong face between her hands, encouraging the intense pressure, boldly meeting his tongue with hers.

With their lips still joined, Dom peeled off her socks. Even that simple gesture stoked the fire, until she thought she would go crazy with the need to be close to him, to have him touching every inch of her skin, to be *part* of him.

Between them they managed to dispense with the remainder of her clothes. The sudden freedom was exhilarating, liberating—naked skin had never felt so wonderful. She twisted her hands into his thick, unruly hair and resumed her loving assault, this time devoting attention to his ear, distracting him as she climbed astride his lap.

A groan struggled to escape his throat, but he kept his mouth shut in an obvious attempt to muffle his pleasure. Dom's tent was in a fairly isolated spot, but sound carried easily in the still night.

She smiled over the effort he made to preserve her reputation—despite the fact that there was little left to protect.

"You think it's funny that you drive me wild?" he asked. He couldn't have seen her smile, for it was too dark, but he must have sensed her amusement. His tone was faintly challenging.

She was about to explain when he grasped her hips and lifted her into position, then lowered her slowly onto his hard, sleek shaft. She bit down on her knuckle to prevent her own outburst of pleasure.

"I th-think it's the other way around," she said in a throaty whisper as he drove inside her body. She twined her arms around his neck and clung to him for support as he lifted her, then pulled her back down, thrusting deeper each time.

"Alicia, oh, sweetheart," he murmured into her hair. "It's all happening so fast again."

"I want it fast," she assured him. "I want it all, now, as hard and fast as it can get."

She had never felt anything so erotic. Within a very short time his hands tightened on her hips. With one final, powerful thrust he reached his peak, just as the pleasure exploded within her. She writhed with the intensity of it. She buried her head against his neck, sure she had dissolved into a pool of pure ecstasy.

Dom was slightly disoriented when he came back to reality. He was sure his soul had left his body for an instant,

the experience had been so intense. If there was such a thing
as heaven on earth, he had surely just lived it.

Gradually he became aware of Alicia's ragged breathing.
He rubbed his cheek against hers and found moisture there,
and all at once a terrible fear was realized. In his uncon-
trollable lust he had hurt her.

"Alicia, I'm so sorry."

"Sorry?" She gave him a throaty laugh. "What on earth
for?"

"Didn't I... hurt you?"

"What? Oh, this." She wiped at her eyes self-consciously.
"Gracious no. You just gave me the ride of my life. Lord,
Dom, couldn't you tell? I thought we were having an earth-
quake."

"I'm afraid I got a little carried away with my own
earthquake," he said, embarrassed. Both times they had
made love, he had missed an event he would very much like
to see. He wanted to watch her face when she reached the
heights of pleasure, and feel her trembling in his arms. "One
of these days I'm going to love you the way you were meant
to be loved."

"You just did." She squeezed him tightly.

"No, I mean... we're going to go slow. I'm going to kiss
every inch of your body and it's going to take... hours."

"Mmm, I'd like that," she said. "How about tonight?"
But her voice had gone drowsy and her eyelids drooped.

"Maybe later," he said, kissing her forehead. She didn't
object as he pulled her off his lap and laid her down on top
of the sleeping bags, cuddling her up against him, her back
to his chest. They slept curled together like spoons.

It was pouring rain the next morning, which gave Dom
and Alicia an excuse to sleep late. Dom woke first, discov-
ering with pleasure the warm woman sleeping next to him on
her stomach. He wished desperately for a palm frond, so he

could pay her back in spades for the way she'd awakened him yesterday.

Since he didn't have one, he lifted her hair and leaned over to kiss the back of her neck. She responded with a lazy sigh, then slowly turned over. The seductive look in her navy-blue eyes was priceless.

She yawned expansively. "It's raining?"

"Uh-huh." He absently rubbed her firm belly with the flat of his hand.

"Does that mean we can stay here all day?"

What a concept, he thought with a surge of longing. "'Fraid not. There's always work to do, rain or shine."

"Are you sure?" She let her hand trail down his chest. The effects of her touch were unmistakable.

With a stab of acute regret he grabbed her wrist and put an end to her mischief. "I'm sure. Decadence is one thing. Letting it interfere with work is another."

"Stick-in-the-mud," she muttered as she sat up, but she softened the barb with a quick kiss before reaching for her clothes.

"What's this?" Dom asked, fingering the small gold locket that dangled between her breasts. He'd noticed it several days ago and had been meaning to ask her about it.

She smiled fondly, then popped it open for him to see. "My mother is on one side, my grandfather on the other. Pretty sappy, huh?"

He shrugged. "My mother wore one very similar. I still have it...somewhere."

There was a long silence as Alicia unself-consciously donned her underclothing. "Your mother died, then?"

He nodded. "I was only two at the time, so I don't remember her at all. She died very suddenly, after a miscarriage."

"I'm sorry," Alicia replied automatically.

He shrugged. "It hit my dad hard. He thought she was invincible—indestructible. For something as normal and everyday as pregnancy to strike her down..." Dom smiled then, surprising Alicia. "Dad used to tell the most amazing stories about her—how she once killed a snake with her bare hands, and how she'd ridden across half of Venezuela on the back of a mule when she was pregnant with me, although she didn't know at the time that she was pregnant. She attributed the morning sickness to some bad meat she'd eaten the day before."

"She must have been quite a woman," Alicia commented.

"Dad used to say she was every bit as tough as he was, and that's pretty tough. For a long time he never even tried to find another wife, because he was sure no other woman could equal her. Then he met Amy..."

"And what happened?" Alicia prompted.

"We both thought she was strong enough, and willing enough, to keep up with the crazy life we led. I have to give her credit for trying—she really did want to please Dad. But then there was the scorpion sting."

"Was it so terrible, what your stepmother did?"

"What do you mean?" Dom asked warily.

"Both times you've mentioned this business with the scorpion, you've gotten this look on your face like...like Amy did something unforgivable. Did she hurt your father?"

Dom looked away, unable to meet Alicia's probing gaze. "Actually, my dad hurt himself. It was his choice to give up archaeology. No, it's what both of them did to me that used to really burn me."

"And what was that?"

"They made *me* give up archaeology."

She stared at him, waiting for him to elaborate, but he didn't. "Obviously you didn't give it up forever," she pointed out. "You're back in the thick of it now. Don't you think it's time to forgive them?"

"I've forgiven them," he assured her. "I know now that they only did what they had to do, to save their marriage. I just didn't adjust to the circumstances very well. It was…is my problem, not theirs."

"What problem is that?" she asked, obviously confused.

He really wasn't sure. "Do we have to talk about this now?" he asked, buying himself some time. She deserved to know. Those events of his childhood had colored his life permanently. But how could he put into words what it felt like to eat, drink and breathe something, then be forced to give it up cold turkey? How could he explain the confusion, the alienation? To put it all into words meant facing his darkest fears straight on, and he wasn't ready for that.

"I didn't mean to pry," she said, and at that moment he knew he loved her for being so compassionate, so undemanding. "I'm just trying to understand you a little better, that's all."

"You understand me better than you think," he said, absently stroking the back of her hand with his thumb. Instinctively she'd known exactly where to probe with her gentle questions. But maybe he needed this. Maybe he needed to be forced to think about all those things he kept pushed to the dustiest corners of his mind.

"I'll drop the subject for now," she said. "But in a few days, I'll bring it up again."

He nodded. Now he would have to face those memories he would rather leave alone. But in doing so, maybe he would get some things straight in his own mind.

The rain had stopped, and Ginny was just putting on the coffee when Alicia and Dom joined her under the house.

"Where's Renaldo?" Dom asked.

"His boat's gone," Ginny answered as she added wood to the fire. "He must have left at dawn."

"In the rain?" Alicia asked, appalled.

"He no doubt knew it would be just a little cloudburst," Dom explained. "Somehow he always knows the weather."

Breakfast was strained as everyone tried to avoid the topic of the new status quo between Dom and Alicia, which most assuredly was common knowledge by now. When they heard a boat motor, Alicia was glad for the distraction.

"That's Renaldo's boat," Dom said, a worried frown drawing his dark eyebrows together. "Now why would he be coming back so soon?"

"Maybe he caught a nice string of fish already," Ginny suggested hopefully. "Mmm, or maybe a barracuda. We haven't had that in a while."

Alicia's stomach turned. She would never truly like fish, although she was learning to tolerate it.

When Renaldo approached the camp, he went directly to Alicia. "I'm afraid I got bad news, lady," he said.

She couldn't imagine what he was talking about, or why he would come to her instead of Dom or Ginny.

By now the others were listening, waiting for his announcement. "About halfway to the village I got a call on my radio. That old man, Del, he was trying to get a message to you."

"Del?" Oh, dear. Perhaps he was sicker than they'd thought.

"He say your grandfather is very ill. You and Skip must come home right away."

Ten

Alicia threw her things into her duffel haphazardly, crying tears of silent rage at the injustice of it all. She had barely scratched the surface of her feelings for Dom, and now she would be forced to leave him, without any mental preparation.

Their relationship had undergone some pretty dramatic changes over the past few days. She couldn't help but wonder what would have happened over the next week if things had been allowed to progress naturally. Now she would never know.

On top of her distress over leaving Dom was the horrible fear that she might lose Eddie J. It would take the better part of a day to get back to Houston. She had no idea how ill her grandfather was: she and Skip might be too late. To lose the two men she loved most in the world, all in one day, would be a crushing blow.

She did love Dom. She'd been fighting that particular emotion, but there was no use denying it any longer. Still, no matter how much she loved him, and even if he returned her love, she had to leave him. If Eddie J. was ill, he would need her more than ever.

It didn't take her long to clean out her tent—she'd brought only as much as she could carry, per Globe Rovers' instructions. She closed all the flaps and called an unfond goodbye down the giant crab hole. "I'd have cooked you for dinner if I could have caught you," she muttered.

As a final gesture she tied her mateless tennis shoe to a tree. She liked the thought of leaving something tangible behind, to remind Dominic of her. Now all she had to do was retrieve the few things she'd put in Dom's tent, and she would be ready—physically, at least—to leave.

She was surprised and grateful to find that Dom had already rolled up her sleeping bag and was letting the air out of her air mattress.

"Thank you—you didn't have to do that," she said.

"I know," he mumbled. "God knows I'm not trying to rush you on your way, but you must be in a hurry."

To avoid looking at him, she dived inside his tent to get her clothes, her flashlight and the few other miscellaneous items she'd left there. She kept her eyes downcast as she stuffed these things into her bag. He handed her the flattened folded air mattress, and she packed it away, too.

Then, abruptly there was nothing left to do. She stood slowly, letting her eyes travel up his jean-clad legs, his narrow hips, his flat belly and chest, those impossibly wide shoulders—and finally his face. In his hazel eyes she saw more pain than she could have imagined.

She spread her hands in a helpless gesture. "It wasn't supposed to end like this."

A brief flash of anger touched his face. "Then tell me, how was it *supposed* to end?" he asked harshly. "Would this be any easier a week down the road?"

"At least we would have been prepared."

"Nothing could have prepared me for this. I wish to hell you'd gone back home that first day."

He couldn't have hurt her more if he'd backhanded her across the face. Tears stung her eyes, and a lump the size of a coconut lodged in her throat. She started to react in anger, but something stopped her. There was a certain familiarity about what he'd just said—not the words themselves, but the emotions behind them.

Then she remembered. He was falling back on the same strategy he'd used that first night, when he'd tried to make her angry rather than face his own feelings.

She met his defiant gaze squarely. "You don't mean that."

He cast his eyes downward, sighing expansively. "You're right, I don't. And I'm sorry—that was a terrible thing to say. I don't regret what's happened between us, even if right now I feel... I don't know. There's not a word for it, I guess." He stuck his thumbs in his pockets and looked around, finally focusing on the pile of her belongings. "Do you need help with that?"

"No, I can manage." She hesitated. "I guess I'd better get going."

"I'll say goodbye here, then, if you don't mind."

She minded saying goodbye, but she was glad for a bit of privacy. With a penitent expression he opened his arms for her and she flew into them, wrapping her own arms around his neck and squeezing for all she was worth. But a warm hug wasn't enough to remember him by.

Her mouth found his, and she kissed him until she was dizzy, until the feel of his hard, demanding lips on hers blocked out all the sadness, the disappointment and the pure, molten fear that she'd never get through the next few hours, or days, or *years,* without him.

She was arousing him, as well as herself. But though their desires would never be fulfilled, she made that kiss everything a kiss could be. When she was hundreds of miles away she would remember the feel of his mouth, his tongue, the unrelenting heat of his body pressed against hers. She hoped he would remember her just as distinctly.

When the sound of Renaldo's boat motor penetrated her haze of emotion, she finally pulled away. "I have to go," she said as her chest rose and fell rapidly.

"I know."

Quickly she threw the straps of her two bags over her shoulder, then picked up her life jacket and rain poncho. She took one last look at him. Oddly, the corner of his mouth had edged up in a half smile.

She turned to go.

"Alicia?"

She stopped, but couldn't look at him again. Her heart pounded wildly and her blood pulsated in her ears. "Yes?"

"Travel safely."

"Yes, I will." She started walking, as quickly as possible, trying to deny the disappointment she felt. What had she expected him to say, that he loved her? *Grow up,* she berated herself. It was time to return to the real world.

She gave Ginny a quick hug before boarding the boat. There was too much to say and no time. But Alicia did unzip her pack and pull out her tube of moisturizer. "A going-away gift," she said.

Ginny smiled her gratitude. "Better than a handful of pure gold."

"The limo should be here in about ten minutes," Skip said. "Jeez, Alicia, you look terrible."

"No matter how terrible I look, I feel worse," she said on a moan. She was slumped in a chair in a passenger lounge at Houston Intercontinental Airport, still fighting the nausea that had plagued her all day. A rough passage to Punta Blanca had started it off; then the tiny, stiflingly hot plane to Belize City had dipped and rocked like a nightmarish amusement park ride. She had begged some motion sickness pills from a fellow traveler at the airport in Belize City, but the medication was too little too late. A bumpy flight from Belize back to the States—plus the aroma of a rubber-chicken airplane meal—had almost finished her off.

Even after landing in Houston, the ordeal hadn't been over. She'd been forced to stand in line for almost an hour to clear Customs. Then Alicia had more or less collapsed in the nearest chair while Skip made some telephone calls to ascertain Eddie J.'s condition. The old man had suffered a stroke—a terrifying piece of news—but the hospital reported him in good condition..

"Why the limo?" she asked. "Why don't we just take a taxi?"

Skip turned up his nose at that idea. "Because, it's going to take excessive luxury and self-pampering to get the taste of Belize out of my mouth. I feel terrible about Eddie J., but I'm sure not glad to be away from that disgusting place."

"Oh, come on, it wasn't *that* bad."

"The hell you say. It was the worst experience of my life . . ." His eyes narrowed calculatingly. "Of course, I can understand why you might not have wanted to leave so soon. You *were* receiving a few exclusive fringe benefits, after all."

Her eyes flew open and she bolted upright, her sudden outrage overshadowing her illness. "Skip, you're such an insensitive ass! If we weren't in a public place I'd punch you right in the nose."

He took a reflexive step backward. "Take it easy, cous. Jeez, you're touchy. I didn't mean anything by it. Did you actually think I'd overlook such a golden opportunity to give you a hard time?''

She shot him a withering look.

"I'm not going to tell anyone else, if that's what you're worried about."

She wilted against her plastic chair, her burst of anger spent. Skip was only teasing her, she supposed. He couldn't understand how his careless words hurt. "Oh, I don't care about that. Tell the whole world, if you want."

"Then what *are* you upset about?" He sat down beside her, placing an awkward hand on her shoulder. "Is it just Eddie J., or something else?"

To her horror, her eyes filled with tears. "It's everything else," she managed to say around the now familiar lump that had returned to her throat. "My whole life looks different than it did a week ago, and I'm not sure how I'm going to cope."

He handed her a bandanna from his back pocket. "Well, then, our expedition wasn't a total loss."

"What do you mean?"

"This trip was supposed to make us reevaluate our priorities, remember? Those were Eddie J.'s exact words."

Alicia laughed despite herself as she dabbed at her watery eyes. "Face it, Skip. In terms of benefiting Bernard Office Products, this trip was a total loss."

He didn't argue with her, but judging from the thoughtful expression on his face, he didn't necessarily agree with her, either. "You want something to eat?" he asked, deftly changing the subject.

The thought of food made her want to retch right then and there, especially since the cloying smell of buttered popcorn permeated the air all over the airport. "No, thanks," she said. "Just lead me to the limo when it gets here. I'll be fine—I think."

The limo driver eyed them both warily a few minutes later as he loaded their filthy luggage into the trunk, then opened the door to allow them into his spotless vehicle. For the first time, Alicia realized how truly awful they looked. They both still wore their mud-smeared rubber boots. Their clothes were none too clean, either. Skip sported a scraggly beard on his sunburned face. Alicia had tucked her impossibly tangled hair under a baseball cap. Her makeupless face was tan as a tomboy's, and she desperately needed a manicure, not to mention a bath.

Once they were seated comfortably, Alicia located a can of club soda in the bar and opened it. The car's interior was cool and the ride whisper smooth, allowing her beleaguered stomach to settle. By the time they arrived at the small, exclusive Oakland Hospital, she felt ready to face whatever came next.

To her surprise, Robert, Del and Peter were waiting for them in the visitor lounge down the hall from Eddie J.'s private room. "How is he?" Alicia immediately asked, gritting her teeth and preparing herself for the worst. "Is he . . . paralyzed?"

"No, just some weakness in his left side," Del answered. "But he has to stay in the hospital a few days for therapy."

"Then he's allowed visitors?" she asked.

Del nodded. "In fact, you just missed your father."

"Oh, darn," Alicia said with absolutely no sincerity. Her father had made very little effort to see her during her childhood. She'd visited him only twice in the past ten years, and they seldom even talked on the phone. They hardly knew each other.

"We haven't been in to see him yet," Peter explained. "He wants to see all the VPs together, as a group. So we've been waiting for you two to get here."

"Let's do it, then," Skip said, fidgeting impatiently.

"Uh, there's just one thing," Peter cautioned as they all made their way down the hall. "Eddie J. doesn't know that some of us came back home ahead of schedule. We sort of didn't tell him."

"You chickens," Alicia berated them, though she couldn't blame them.

"Well, it's about time," came a surprisingly strident voice as they all entered the spacious room. "The old general is stricken with a mortal illness, and it takes his troops a day and a half to reach him. Don't you want to hear my dying wishes?"

"Dying!" Alicia said, her skepticism clear. "You old reprobate, you're not anywhere near dying. If you looked any healthier you'd be out running a marathon." She softened her sharp remark with a kiss to the old man's sandpapery cheek, much relieved to see that he really did look pretty good. She wouldn't have been surprised to see him get up out of bed and go to work.

But he couldn't, she had to remind herself, or he wouldn't be in this bed in the first place. She'd never known him to be sick, and seeing him in this place was unnerving.

"So... sorry to cut your trip short," he said cheerfully.

"We're not," Skip mumbled, which caused Eddie J. to eye him carefully. Then he looked at all of them more closely—Peter's bandaged hand, Robert's angry welts from the bug bites, Skip's sunburn, Alicia's dishevel—and his clear blue eyes widened in surprise. "Good God Almighty, what *happened* to you people? Would you like to join me here? I could have a few extra beds moved in."

"Coconut Cay was a *horrible* place," Peter suddenly exclaimed. "There's no fresh water, no electricity—"

"No decent place to sleep," said Del.

"No decent food," Robert added. "The sand flies ate me alive." Then they were all talking at once.

"I burned my hand on the coffeepot."

"I got so stressed out I thought I was having a heart attack, and my arthritis—"

"You wouldn't believe the mud, and the scorpions—"

"Snakes," someone added, which was a blatant lie. No one had seen any snakes.

"What a bunch of pantywaists!" Eddie J. said with a derisive curl of his lip. Then he looked at Alicia, the only one of his vice presidents who had remained silent. "Well, girl, aren't you going to add any complaints to the list?"

She shrugged. "I liked it." This caused a chorus of objections from her co-workers. "I did like it," she insisted.

"She liked the archaeologist," Skip said under his breath, just loud enough that she could hear. She stepped on his toe, producing a satisfying yelp of protest.

"Did you accomplish *anything* worthwhile?" Eddie J. demanded.

Skip stepped forward. "Well, sir," he said, as if on the verge of bowing and scraping. "I have to admit that the whole expedition was pretty much a wash. We were so busy trying to survive that I'm afraid we didn't accomplish any of our goals."

"That's not quite true," Alicia objected. "I figured out what the problem is at work. It's me."

Everyone stared at her.

"I realized something about myself," she elaborated. "As the company's gotten larger I've become more and more frustrated. There's more red tape. Everything takes longer. I can't see the results of my work as quickly. And I've taken out my frustration on all of you. I've interfered in your departments, and I've been generally difficult. I owe you all an apology."

Their eyes grew wider and their jaws dropped lower.

"How did making mud pies and slapping at insects give you such insight?" Skip finally asked.

"The work was satisfying in a way that my work at Bernard Office Products hasn't been in a long time." She watched Eddie J. carefully, to see how he would react to her admission. His eyes flickered with interest, no more. She shrugged. "Anyway, I'll try to be better," she ended lamely.

A nurse entered the room just then. She skidded to a stop, staring in horror at the ragged-looking visitors. "You can't all stay in here," she said sternly as she stepped through the group toward Eddie J.'s bed, to check his vital signs. "You'll have to leave. One visitor at a time."

"Oh, simmer down, Josie," he cajoled the stout, middle-aged nurse, speaking around the thermometer stuck in his mouth. "I'm having a managers' meeting. It's important."

She lifted one eyebrow skeptically.

"Give us five more minutes," he said.

She nodded reluctantly, made a few notations on his chart, then left them in peace.

He cleared his throat importantly. "All right, let's get down to business. My doctor informs me that the stroke I suffered was a minor one. So no, I'm not dying. But I've been told in no uncertain terms that I have to slow down. It probably won't come as a shock to you to hear that I'm retiring, effective immediately. Now I have to name my choice to succeed me, subject to the board's approval, of course."

"Then you were testing us," Skip said.

Eddie J.'s bushy white eyebrows drew together in confusion. "What? What are you talking about, son?"

"Um, it's just that I thought you'd choose a new CEO based on our performance in Belize," Skip mumbled.

Eddie J. rolled his eyes. "I made my decision months ago, you idiot," he said. "Surely the choice must be obvious. Del's been with me for more than twenty years. He knows the operation inside and out."

Alicia grinned with relief, shooting Del an I-told-you-so look. Everyone else was too surprised to do much of anything.

The nurse stuck her head back in the room. "Out," she ordered. "If Dr. Clinton finds you in here he'll skin me."

"Better do as she says," Eddie J. said with a chuckle. "She's a mean one. But you can stay a few minutes, Alicia. I'd like to talk to you alone."

The request filled her with apprehension. He probably wanted her to elaborate on the job frustration she'd mentioned earlier. He had always been very sensitive to any dissatisfaction among his employees, and she had no doubts that he would do anything within his power to ensure that she enjoyed her work.

"So," he began. "Bernard Office Products has gotten too big for your taste?"

"I didn't mean it the way it sounded," she hastened to explain. "I simply need to make some adjustments, that's all. It's nothing but growing pains, no reason to—"

"You're not happy," he said flatly.

"Of course I'm happy." Her assurance sounded hollow, even to her own ears, and Eddie J. narrowed his eyes thoughtfully.

"Alicia," he said after a long pause, "you can be frank with me. I've known for a long time that you were dissatisfied. I could have lain many of the problems at work right on your doorstep, but I didn't want to do that. I wanted you to discover for yourself that you were causing friction, and I think you have."

She nodded.

"I'd hoped that a break in the routine would set everything aright, but it didn't. What's it going to take to make you smile again?"

"I want…I want to work more with my hands," she said hesitantly. "I want to see the results of my labor. I want to go to bed each night knowing I've accomplished something. It used to be so exciting, knowing that the company was growing and becoming prosperous as a direct result of my efforts. But now everything's so..."

"Boring?" Eddie J. offered.

She didn't answer, but he'd hit the proverbial nail on the head.

"Then get out. For God's sake, quit Bernard. Change careers. Travel—you've got the money."

She was shaking her head in denial. "No, no, I could never leave you. I could never leave the company. That's my whole life, my dream."

"The company was *my* dream, sweetheart. You were caught up in my enthusiasm. But you've got to follow *your* dream, now. And none of this nonsense about loyalty. Bernard needed you once, but there are plenty of engineers out there that can handle your job—people with energy and excitement to spare. What Del doesn't need is a vice president who doesn't really care anymore."

She swallowed, hard. As usual, her grandfather had cut right to the quick with his canny observations.

"Quit, girl. If you don't, I'll see that you're fired."

Dom sat on the trunk of a fallen tree and stared out over the aquamarine waters of the Gulf of Honduras, toward the mainland. He'd taken to doing that a lot during the past week, for in that direction was the last glimpse he'd gotten of Alicia, sitting in the front of Renaldo's dory. He had watched until the boat was out of sight. She hadn't looked back, not once.

Another group of volunteers was due to arrive tomorrow. The activity around Coconut Cay would pick up, which hopefully would distract him from his melancholy. But he wasn't really sure anything would remove the evocative memory of Alicia from his brain. He recalled the exact texture of her skin, her hair, the musical sound of her voice and the way those incredible navy-blue eyes could snap with anger one minute and melt with passion the next. He was half afraid her memory would haunt him always. But the alternative—having the memory fade—would be much worse.

He slapped at a sand fly on his bare arm. "Damned nuisance," he muttered. This island could be pretty unfriendly. If fate had given him the time he needed, he would have asked Alicia to stay here with him. She might have even agreed, for she always managed to surprise him. But that wouldn't have been fair, he realized now—no more fair than it would have been for his father to insist that Amy stay with him in Tunisia. A woman like Alicia deserved a better world, a softer, less-punishing place. Even as that thought formed, he realized he was categorizing her again.

"Want some of this?" Ginny asked. She'd come up quietly behind him, and he jumped at the sound of her voice. She was holding out the tube of Alicia's moisturizer. "I noticed you've been slapping at those cursed bugs."

"No, I don't want any," he snapped. "And I wish you wouldn't use it, either."

"What? Are you nuts, Dominic? This is the only product we've ever found that works to keep the sand flies off. Why would you—"

"Because the scent reminds me of her," he cut in. He hadn't realized that until after she was gone. Now even the slightest whiff of the stuff squeezed at his heart until he could hardly breathe.

"Oh," Ginny said. Then, "Ohhh." She sat down on the tree beside him, though he hadn't invited her. But now that she was here, he intended to ask her something.

"You're a woman," he began.

"You're just now noticing?"

He ignored her ribbing. "You like it here, don't you?"

"Well . . . I like the work, but amenities leave a lot to be desired. There are times I'd kill to be able to hop in my car and buzz down to the 7-11. Sometimes I wish I could put on makeup and do my hair and go out for dinner and dancing. But most of the time I like it here okay."

"What about Alicia? Do you think she could learn to like it?"

"Lord, Dom, you've got it pretty bad for that girl."

He didn't bother to deny it.

"I assumed it was just a case of lust," she continued bluntly. "I thought that as soon as she was gone, you'd get back to normal. How long are you going to moon about like this? We have a lot of work to get done."

"I know. And I'm not going to 'moon about,' as you so quaintly put it, for much longer."

"Well thank goodness."

"I'm going after her."

"You're *what?*" Ginny nearly fell off the tree trunk in shock.

"I'm going to Houston, and I'm going to find her, and I'm going to convince her that we should be together. If not here, then there."

"Houston? But you couldn't live in—"

"I will if that's what it takes." And he would be doing exactly what his father had done, the very thing he'd sworn he would never do. But now, finally, he truly understood what had made his father give up his fieldwork. He loved Amy, above all else. For that kind of love a man can make sacrifices. And in the end maybe changing his life-style wouldn't be the soul-crushing kind of sacrifice Dom had once envisioned. With Alicia to help him, he could learn other ways, other work that would satisfy him the way archaeology once had.

"But how could you give up all this?" Ginny asked, indicating with a bold sweep of her hand the mud, the dilapidated house and the swarm of tiny insects that preyed on them.

"Once I didn't think I could," he said, giving the question a more serious answer than it deserved. "But burying myself in my work and isolating myself from the rest of the world isn't as desirable as I've always thought. I've been missing a few things. A lot of people have tried to tell me that, even Renaldo." Dom laughed softly. "He said my little bits of pottery and bones couldn't keep me warm at night. He was right."

"When will you leave?" Ginny asked, accepting the inevitable.

"Tomorrow."

"Tomorrow!" she screeched. "We have a dozen volunteers arriving tomorrow. Just what do you expect me to do with them?"

"Ah, hell, Ginny, you know this island and this project better than I do. You'll have two grad students to help, too. Just . . . proceed."

"When will you be back?"

"Maybe never."

Eleven

Dom sat on the screened-in porch of the Mahogany Beach Hotel, trying to relax and enjoy the amenities, such as they were. The Mahogany Beach was no luxury resort—in fact, it was distinctly run-down. But it was clean, the staff was pleasant and the food hearty. At any rate, it was one of the best Belize City had to offer, and he encouraged all his volunteers to stay here whenever they had a layover in this less-than-charming town.

Right now it felt good to sit in a real chair with a cushion and a back, and sip a good, strong rum and Coke from a real glass. Many of the hotel's guests spent the evening here on the dimly lit porch, taking advantage of the cooling sea breeze.

Stranded in Belize City overnight due to flight schedules, Dom had killed an afternoon by buying a few new clothes to spruce up his image. He'd even gotten a haircut and a barbershop shave. He didn't want to arrive on Alicia's doorstep looking like some unkempt savage. What was appropriate on Coconut Cay could offend delicate sensibilities in the city.

It had occurred to him, more than once, that he might be making a fool of himself. Suppose he and Alicia were merely victims of their wild environment. With the trade winds to stir their libidos into a frenzy, and with the sun and clear blue waters and quiet, starlit skies adding to the mood, desire was bound to blossom. Would they run into trouble when they exchanged their tropical paradise for the real, everyday world? Could their relationship transcend the harsh realities of earning a living, taking out the garbage and paying the bills?

In a civilized world, would their untamed passions fizzle?

Dom didn't think so, and he was willing to risk finding out. Anyway, Coconut Cay was hardly paradise, despite its occasional lovely moments.

A tinkle of musical laughter drifted to his ears from the other end of the long porch. The sound reminded him of Alicia. Of course, most everything reminded him of Alicia. A shiny black bird's wing made him think of her hair. The softness of a flower's petal called to mind her skin. He'd seen a scarf in a shop window today and had impulsively bought it for her, simply because the deep blue color would exactly match her eyes.

The laughter sounded again. This time he turned his head, and his heart did a half gainer. It couldn't be. He must be hallucinating. But it *was*. Alicia Bernard, or her twin sister, sat not thirty feet away from him.

When his heart started to beat again, the tempo had doubled. His palms grew moist and his head spun. What was she doing here? He wasn't ready to face her yet. How would he explain his presence here, when he was supposed to be on the island?

This certainly threw a wrench into his plans. It was a cinch he couldn't just sit here and wait for her to blunder into him on her way to her room. He had to confront her.

Inspiration struck, and he motioned toward the waiter with a wave of his hand.

"Yes, sir?" the polite young man asked.

"Ricky, could you deliver a cold glass of Chablis to the woman in the flowered dress—the one at the end of the porch? And I'd like to send a note with it."

Ricky winked conspiratorially. "Yes, sir. Let me get the drink, and I come back for the note."

Dom pulled a pen from the pocket of his new, crisp cotton shirt and scribbled a short missive on his cocktail napkin.

Alicia looked up to see the young waiter standing next to her chair, bearing a glass of wine.

"Chablis," he said. "Compliments of the gentleman at the other end of the porch."

"Oh, how nice," she said noncommittally. She wasn't in the mood to deal with a pick-up attempt this evening. Still, she supposed she owed the man some sort of acknowledgment, even though she was tired to the bone and anxious over tomorrow's confrontation with Dom. She had no idea how he would deal with her unannounced return to Coconut Cay, much less the declaration of her feelings she intended to make.

She returned her attention to the wine, taking a sip. "Mmm. How did he know I like Chablis?" she wondered aloud, addressing her question toward the elderly couple she'd been conversing with.

"He also give you this," the waiter said, handing her a napkin before leaving her to ponder the message.

She felt a rush of heat in her face as she read the bold suggestion.

"What does it say?" the gray-haired woman asked.

Alicia answered the question with one of her own. "What kind of jerk would suggest a hot shower and a bed with soft sheets to a complete strange—" She nearly choked on her words as their familiarity struck home—cold Chablis, hot shower, clean bed with soft sheets. Only one person had heard her make that errant request, when she was marooned on a deserted island.

"Dom?" The name was scarcely whispered as she peered down the dimly lit porch. But that wasn't Dom. She couldn't see his face, but still, it couldn't be Dom. This man wore a tailored shirt with cuffs, and real trousers. His dark hair was neatly trimmed, his face clean shaven. But when he turned his head, she recognized the strong countenance that would forever be etched into her memory.

He smiled uncertainly at her.

She wasn't about to question fate. With the wineglass still clutched in her hand, she catapulted herself out of her chair and rushed across the length of the porch. No sooner had Dom stood up than she landed squarely against his hard chest. Her arms went around him and she spilled wine down his back, but he didn't seem to mind.

"I can't believe you're really here," he said just before his lips found hers. A titter of amusement sounded from the other hotel guests on the porch, but Alicia didn't care. Dom was here, she was in his arms again, and for now that was all that mattered.

He deepened the kiss, holding her closer, touching her more intimately. The fingertips of one hand grazed the side of her breast; his other hand curved possessively around her hip. She had to do something before they really put on a show.

Reluctantly she pulled her mouth away from him. "Did you say something about a shower and a soft bed?" she whispered discreetly.

He made a sort of growling noise in response, which she took for an affirmative answer.

"Let me get my purse." She extracted herself from his embrace. In the time it took her to walk to the other end of the porch, retrieve her handbag and bid the curious elderly couple a hasty good-night, she cooled off enough to come to her senses. She couldn't just jump into bed with Dom. They had a few things to discuss—like whether they had a future.

No words were exchanged between them as they walked hand in hand to Dom's room. He still said nothing as he turned on the light, closed the door quietly behind them and switched on the ceiling fan. She stood awkwardly just inside the room, searching for the right words to tell him of her intentions.

He took the empty wineglass from her hand and set it on the battered dresser. Next he slipped the shoulder strap of her purse down her arm and set the bag aside. Finally he took her hand and led her to the bed. Since her knees didn't want to hold her up much longer, anyway, she sank onto the mattress when he gave her a gentle push.

"Now," he said, standing before her, "what'll it be first? The shower or the bed?" He smiled wickedly. "Either choice, you'll have to take me with you."

An objection was on the tip of her tongue. But somehow, she just couldn't bring up a subject that might ruin the mood. She wanted this night with him too badly.

She took a deep breath, then blurted out her most honest and immediate feelings. "Bed. I can't think of anything else right now."

Her words caused a light of anticipation to flash in his eyes. She expected him to take her in his arms again and reignite the flash fire of passion that had started out on the porch. Instead, he knelt down and began to unbuckle one of her white sandals. He slid the shoe off, then slowly massaged her bare foot, letting his fingers trail up and down her calf. He repeated the procedure with her other foot, and she let him, simply because his touch felt too good to interrupt.

When he finished his slow massage, he ran one hand up her leg, dipping briefly under the full skirt of her cabbage-rose dress to caress her knee before continuing upward on top of the fabric—up her thigh, her hip, her waist. She could feel his warmth through the thin material of her snug bodice as his hand crept up her rib cage, stopping just beneath her breast. She thought her heart would stop, too. What was he doing to her?

He kissed her chastely, on the corner of her mouth, then let his lips graze down her cheek, along the line of her jaw, to her ear. All the while she sat very still, practically gasping for air, resisting the urge to just grab him and devour him with her own kisses. What was he waiting for? Surely he wanted her as badly as she did him.

He removed her clip earrings with gentle hands—first one, then the other, hardly touching her. He performed the task almost as a ritual, which made her feel like a virgin being prepared for sacrifice. The notion first amused her, then made her tingle with anticipation.

"Dom, what are you doing?" she finally asked, her voice a breathy whisper.

"We're going to do it right this time," he said just before leaning in to kiss her neck. He traced his tongue lightly along her collarbone, making it nearly impossible for her to voice her next question.

"You mean we...we didn't do it right the first two times?"

She felt, rather than heard, the chuckle of amusement that caused a puff of his breath to ruffle her hair. "Maybe I should say, we're going to do it *slow* this time."

Just the way he said *slooowwww* caused heat to bloom inside her—in the pit of her stomach, then lower, in her abdomen and at the very source of her womanliness.

He reached behind her to unzip her summery dress, one divine inch at a time. When the bodice was open to her waist he pulled it forward and down, revealing the cool cotton undershirt that barely covered her breasts. She hadn't purposely dressed to beguile anyone that day; her costume had been calculated to battle the oppressive tropical heat. But apparently it impressed Dom, for he breathed in great ragged gulps of air as he pulled her to her feet and slipped the dress down her hips and legs.

He stepped back to admire her, now clad only in the undershirt and skimpy bikini briefs. Under his appreciative gaze, her nipples hardened into taut peaks, clearly visible through the thin fabric that stretched across them.

Some small part of her, the part that had once been a shy virgin, wanted to turn off the lights and dive under the covers. She found it much easier to be brazen on a wild, jungle-choked island than here, with the trappings of civilization all around them. On the island certain events beyond her control had influenced her behavior, causing her to feel and act like someone apart from herself. Here she was definitely Alicia Bernard.

She dropped her chin and folded her arms across her breasts, suddenly embarrassed.

"Don't," he beseeched, stepping close once again to gently unfold her arms from their self-protective position. "You're so beautiful. Let me look at you."

The awkward moment passed. In his eyes she saw all the reassurance she could possibly want. This man cared for her, and whatever the future held, tonight was theirs, and it was right. She reached up to stroke his smooth face. With a hand at the back of his neck, she guided him home for another kiss, this one deep and wet and utterly erotic, so that she couldn't help but press her body up against his. His clothing hampered her pleasure, and she could only wish she'd had the sense to divest him earlier.

She plunged her hands between them and worked at his shirt buttons, but in her agitation she fumbled and failed miserably. He grabbed her wrists and stilled her efforts.

"I'll take care of that," he whispered, making quick work of the buttons. "In fact, I'll take care of everything ... this time."

She sensed that he had a definite scenario in mind. Whatever it was, she knew she would enjoy it. So she sat meekly on the bed and watched him undress, content to let him run the whole show ... this time.

She marveled anew at his perfect male body—so hard and lean, virtually vibrating with suppressed power and raw virility. Just the sight of him, peeling his khaki slacks off his sinewy thighs, caused her to bite her own lip with the force of her aching need. To her minor disappointment, he didn't take quite *everything* off. But she, too, was still partially clothed, which left a few delicious possibilities for later.

Without using words, he urged her to lie back on the old mahogany bed.

What now? she wondered as a sharp thrill zipped up her spine.

He sat on the edge of the bed next to her, and for a few moments he just looked at her, like a starving man contemplating the feast of his dreams. Then, to her surprise, he took her hand and brought it to his mouth, lightly grazing the knuckles with his lips.

"I want you to know I've never done this before," he said.

"Done what?" she asked, perplexed.

"Made love to a woman. I don't mean sex," he said when she opened her mouth to object. "Obviously I've done that. I'm talking about loving every part of a woman's body,

learning where to touch, where to kiss, how to drive her—
you, I mean—absolutely wild. Ever since the first night we
were together I've thought about this, about how I wanted
to go about it if I ever got the chance. I hope you'll give me
that chance. I don't know exactly what I'm doing, but I'm
willing to learn.''

"Oh, Dom." What woman could turn down a request like
that? She quickly blinked back tears of sweet emotion.
"You can make love to me any way you like." She knew that
any manner in which he chose to touch her would be exquisite, no matter how unschooled in lovemaking he claimed to
be.

With the lights out, his gentle assault on her senses soon
caused her to wonder about that claim. By pure instinct he
knew her body better than she did. As he trailed kisses and
caresses up and down her legs, behind her knees and on her
sensitive inner thigh, he found places that triggered incredible responses from her—places she never even knew ex-
isted.

When he had exhausted every possibility from her toes to
her hips, he shifted his attention to her midriff, pushing her
undershirt above her breasts and out of his way so he could
shower hot kisses along her ribs and abdomen. He teased
her navel with his tongue, and she squealed in pure delight.

"Did that tickle?" he asked, concerned.

"Not . . . not exactly. Oh, Lord, Dom, don't stop."

He didn't. Skipping over her breasts for the moment, he
focused on her hands, the inside of her wrists and elbows,
her shoulders. When he finally did let his mouth wander to
her hard nipple, almost as if by accident, she groaned her
approval. Her fingers wound their way through the strangely
short strands of his hair, urging him in no uncertain terms
to continue.

He allowed her to hold him captive there for a little longer, then pulled away. She made a sound that might have been surprise or dismay or disappointment.

"Make love to me now," she asked in a small voice.

"That's what I'm doing." He began to nibble on her neck.

She sighed longingly, even as she lovingly caressed his chest. "You know what I mean."

"I'm getting to that." Loving her in this leisurely fashion was proving to be heady stuff. But he wasn't sure how much was too much of a good thing—he wanted her aroused, not so frustrated that she was tempted to bash him over the head with the bedside lamp. So he moved as if to fulfill her request, sliding his fingers under the elastic of her panties and slowly pulling them down her legs.

Her impatience was almost palpable. Still, he had no intention of cutting his fantasy short. He urged her silky thighs apart and kissed her most intimate, secret places.

She tensed at first. "What are you—" she started to say, but a moan of ecstasy overruled the objection. Her every intake of breath excited him; every syllable she uttered— whether it made sense or not—made him burn with the desire to please her. To think that he could bring her so much pleasure doing something so wildly fun for himself was euphoric.

He knew when she neared her peak. He could feel her trembling, then a sudden tension, then the intense spasms of release. Witnessing her climax was one of the most amazing experiences of his life.

When she was at last still, he pulled himself up and rested his head on her belly. She stroked his damp hair as her breathing slowed.

Her voice shook when she spoke. "I thought you said you didn't know what you were doing."

"I didn't."

"Could have fooled me. Are you sure you don't have an owner's manual to my body hidden somewhere around here?"

He laughed, and his breath tickled her stomach. The ceiling fan cooled her slick skin, and she shivered.

"Cold?" he asked. "How about that hot shower?"

"You're not suggesting we're done, are you?"

"I certainly hope not."

A shower sounded divine. At any rate, Alicia was too spent to object when Dom peeled off her undershirt and his briefs, then whisked her into the bathroom. He practically had to prop her up against the wall of the tiny shower—her legs wouldn't support her. But the trickle of warm water soon revived her, and the vigorous soaping Dom gave her body did other, more delicious things to her. Before she knew what was happening they were kissing again. His soap-slippery skin felt incredibly sensuous to the touch, and she touched it all over, with every part of her body.

She gave a shriek of surprise and delight when he leaned back against the shower wall and lifted her up, coaxing her to wrap her legs around his hips. He entered her that way. And though their union was short-lived, it was sweetly intense.

Minutes later they lay together on the cool sheets, letting the ceiling fan dry them as they reveled in a particularly poignant afterglow.

"So what are you doing in Belize City?" Dom finally asked.

"I was wondering when you'd get around to that. I could ask you the same question."

"I, uh, had business to take care of."

"So did I," she said.

"What kind of business?"

"Personal business. There's this man, you see, whom I'm wildly in love with, and I came here to declare my intentions."

His hand, resting indolently on her hip, suddenly gripped her tightly. "You love me?"

"Yes." The declaration had been surprisingly easy. "I hope that doesn't scare you."

"Scare me? Honey, I was terrified that you *didn't* feel the way I did. I was on my way to Houston to see you. That's the business I had to take care of. I want to be with you, Alicia, always. I'm sure I could get a teaching job somewhere in Houston. Even if it takes a while to find the right position, I have quite a nest egg built up—"

"Wait a minute, we aren't going to live in Houston."

"We aren't?"

"Oh, Dom, I would never ask or expect that of you. You said it would destroy you."

"Maybe I ought to explain why I felt that way," he said. It was a few moments before he spoke again. Collecting all his thoughts on this sensitive subject took some time. "When Dad stopped his fieldwork to be with Amy, I was forced to give up the only life I knew. It was devastating. I never fit in with the kids in that small town. Nothing they said or did made a bit of sense to me. It was like a foreign language. I floundered. For five years I was miserably out of place.

"But... maybe I never tried to fit in. Dad made the adjustment because he had Amy. He had something to fill the void. I understand that now.

"And I'll have you to help me make the adjustment. You'll make me want to learn a new way of living. It'll be a challenge, and that couldn't possibly hurt me."

She pressed her cheek against his chest, and he realized she was crying. "You really do love me, don't you," she said softly. "To make such a sacrifice—"

"Of course I love you. How could I not? And living the rest of my life with you is no sacrifice. It's settled, then."

She raised her head to look at him, teary eyed but smiling mischievously. "Not quite. We can't go back to Houston. There's nothing there for me. I quit my job, sublet my apartment, sold my car and my furniture. The sum total of my earthly belongings are stacked in a room down the hall."

Dom blinked a couple of times, then fell back against the pillows, too stunned to respond for a moment. "You quit your job?"

"Or I was fired—depends on how you look at it. My grandfather realized even before I did that I'd given everything I had to give to Bernard Office Products and it was time for me to move on."

"Your grandfather—damn, I forgot. Is he all right? I'm sorry I didn't ask earlier."

"He's out of the hospital and doing very well, and don't change the subject. Will you let me stay and work with you on the excavation? My engineering skills could come in quite handy, you know. I could whip that house into shape. And during the flight over here I was thinking of a way to collect rain water and heat it using solar energy. We could have hot, fresh-water showers. Just imagine!"

"Alicia, you don't have to sell me on your usefulness. But...you *hate* it here."

She shook her head. "No I don't."

"You even said you did," he argued. "You hate fish and coconuts and boats...and mud and bugs and crabs—"

"Oh, that. I was just throwing a temper tantrum. That's the way I release stress. I'd almost drowned, remember. I had to blow off some steam somehow. I didn't mean any of that stuff I said. Dom, I *love* that crazy island, bugs and all. It's exhilarating, and it stretches me to the very boundaries of my abilities. And you're there, which makes everything all right. I'm even acquiring a taste for seafood."

"You're saying you'll stay there the rest of the digging season?" he asked incredulously.

She nodded. "And then I'll go anywhere else you'd like to go—South America, Egypt, the North Pole for all I care. I just want to be with you. I'm tougher than I look—haven't I proved that?"

He frowned. She was handing him a dream come true— the love of a lifetime and the freedom to continue his work as he always had, with her at his side. But suddenly that didn't seem enough.

"What's wrong?" she asked worriedly.

"What about a home? Stability? Babies?"

Her eyebrows flew up. "Babies?" she repeated.

"We can't be dragging small children all over the world with us. When they're older, sure, but—"

Alicia laughed. "Shall I assume your failure to mention marriage before babies was merely an oversight?"

"Oh, uh, right. We are going to get married, aren't we?"

She nodded enthusiastically.

"All right. Now that that's settled, I suppose we could live in Tucson. At least I'm already on the payroll at the university there, but my apartment is terrible—we'd have to buy a house."

"You actually have an apartment?"

"Well, I have to stop now and then to write up my findings, do my income taxes—"

"See there? We can have it all. We can travel and work together sometimes, we can stay home and be domestic at other times, and I'm sure we can squeeze in a baby or two."

"Oh, Alicia, you are something else. You make it sound so... possible."

"Of course it's possible. We are two very amazing people. We can do anything we put our minds to."

He kissed her tenderly, suddenly secure in the knowledge that their life together would be stimulating and satisfying, no matter how they worked things out. The specifics no longer mattered.

As he held her, feeling their hearts beating in tandem, he thought of the many exciting moments his archaeology had brought to his life—the many wonderful treasures he'd brought forth from the earth. But no matter how exciting, no earthly find could compare with the unearthly delights of Alicia's love.

* * * * *

SET SAIL FOR THE SOUTH SEAS
with
BESTSELLING AUTHOR
EMILIE RICHARDS

In September Silhouette Sensation begins a very special mini-series by a very special author. *Tales of the Pacific*, by Emilie Richards, will take you to Hawaii, New Zealand and Australia and introduce you to a group of men and women you will never forget.

The *Tales of the Pacific* are four stories of love as lush as the tropics, as deep as the sea and as enduring as the sky above. They are coming your way—only in Silhouette Sensation!

COMING NEXT MONTH

TEARS OF THE ROSE
B J James

To the world, Jordana Daniels had it all. Few knew
of the reclusive cover girl's past or the shocking
secret with which she lived. But one man was
destined to learn the truth . . .

A LITTLE TIME IN TEXAS
Joan Johnston

Texas in 1864 was no place for a lady on her own,
but having a rough and rugged stranger pull her into
the twentieth century was beyond belief! What was
the future for Angela Taylor and Texas Ranger
Dallas Masterson?

TALK OF THE TOWN
Beverly Barton

Lydia Reid had never been the subject of scandal,
unlike her unfaithful late husband. But when
country boy Wade Cameron befriended her the
whole town began talking . . .

Silhouette Desire

COMING NEXT MONTH

UPON THE STORM
Justine Davis

Trace Dalton had spent three years searching for Christy Reno. But Christy could never be part of his world so she was going to hold fast to what she had—even if it meant losing the only man she'd ever loved.

ROUGH AND READY
Leslie Davis Guccione

Dory Lydon thought men were about as trustworthy as snakes, so when she ran into six feet, two inches of green-eyed anger in the form of a broad-shouldered, narrow-hipped, ranch foreman, instinct told her to keep her distance!

WHERE THERE IS LOVE
Annette Broadrick

Secret agent Max Moran had ended Marisa Stevens' career. Why was she asking for his help now? They had to rescue a child, but desire had been simmering for six years . . . Could they still work together?

BARBARY WHARF
BOOK 5

Now that Gib and Valerie have found each other, what is to become of Guy Faulkner, the *Sentinel* lawyer, and Sophie Watson his secretary, both rejected and abandoned by the people they loved.

Could they find solace together, or was Sophie at least determined not to fall in love on the rebound, even if Guy did seem to think it was time for him to find true love?

Find out in Book 5 of Barbary Wharf —

A SWEET ADDICTION

Available: September 1992   Price: £2.99

W●RLDWIDE